PRAISE FOR
ANNABELLE DIXON COZY MYSTERY SERIES

"Absolutely wonderful!!"
"Like visiting friends that you want to visit with as much as possible."
"I read it that night, and it was GREAT!"
"I couldn't put it down!"
"4 thumbs up!!!"
"It kept me up until 3am. I love it."
"As a former village vicar this ticks the box for me."
"This series keeps getting better and better."
"Annabelle, with her great intuition, caring personality, yet imperfect judgement, is a wonderful main character."
"It's fun to grab a cup of tea and pretend I'm sitting in the vicarage discussing the latest mysteries with Annabelle whilst she polishes off the last of the cupcakes."
"Great book - love Reverend Annabelle Dixon and can't wait to read more of her books."
"Annabelle reminds me of Agatha Christie's Miss Marple."
"Cozy mystery done very well."
"I LOVE ANNABELLE!"

"A wonderful read, delightful characters and if that's not enough the sinfully delicious recipes will have you coming back for more."

"This cozy series is a riot!"

GRAVE IN THE GARAGE

BOOKS IN THE REVEREND ANNABELLE DIXON SERIES

Chaos in Cambridge (Prequel)

Death at the Café

Murder at the Mansion

Body in the Woods

Grave in the Garage

Horror in the Highlands

Killer at the Cult

Fireworks in France

Witches at the Wedding

COLLECTIONS

Books 1-4

Death at the Café

Murder at the Mansion

Body in the Woods

Grave in the Garage

Books 5-7

Horror in the Highlands

Killer at the Cult

Fireworks in France

GRAVE IN THE GARAGE

ALISON GOLDEN

JAMIE VOUGEOT

The characters and events portrayed in this book are fictitious. Any similarity to real persons, living or dead is coincidental and not intended by the author.

Text copyright © 2016 Alison Golden

All rights reserved.

No part of this book may be reproduced, stored in a retrieval system, or transmitted in any form or by any means, electronic, mechanical, photocopying, recording, or otherwise, without express written permission of the publisher.

Published by Mesa Verde Publishing
P.O. Box 1002
San Carlos, CA 94070

ISBN: 978-1537324142

"Some books leave us free and some books make us free."
- Ralph Waldo Emerson -

"Your emails seem to come on days when I need to read them because they are so upbeat."
- Linda W -

For a limited time, you can get the first books in each of my series - *Chaos in Cambridge, Hunted* (exclusively for subscribers - not available anywhere else), *The Case of the Screaming Beauty,* and *Mardi Gras Madness* - plus updates about new releases, promotions, and other Insider exclusives, by signing up for my mailing list at:

https://www.alisongolden.com/annabelle

CHAPTER ONE

THE USUAL FEELINGS of peace and tranquility that beset Annabelle whenever she walked around St. Mary's centuries-old graveyard were not present today. She walked slowly between the decrepit, leaning stones, avoiding patches of sodden, forlorn grass that even a cow would turn its nose up at, her feet heavy as they crunched dry leaves underfoot. She shivered and pulled her black cassock tighter around her, not yet accustomed to the wintery chill.

Her time as vicar at St. Mary's church had been a consistent, daily process of rejuvenation; spiritually, socially, and not least, architecturally. Annabelle had taken every care to ensure that the church was a wonderful and pleasing tribute to the Lord. From the luxurious velvet of the kneeling cushions to the inch-perfect preservation of its roof tiles, Annabelle was sure He would be proud. Shrubbery and other flora that ran all around the church had been carefully groomed into a flourishing yet orderly arrangement—a delightful array of coloured blossoms in summer, a thick display of sculpted, earthy tones in winter. Annabelle had even varnished the mahogany pews and tenderly polished the stained glass windows herself.

The graveyard, however, had remained an untouched thorn in Annabelle's side. All its residents were a few generations dead, their descendants long since moved away or neglectful in the upkeep of their deceased relative's crumbling resting places. Annabelle had ignored the cemetery during her persistent improvements to the church, partly because she loathed to disrupt the timeworn dignity of the area, partly because she had always favoured life and vitality over the solemnity of death. But now that the graveyard had taken on a wild, unrestrained, almost ghoulish appearance, she could no longer delay addressing its deterioration.

Moss and trailing plants covered many of the gravestones. Some of them so much so that even the names and dates, carefully engraved on them once upon a time, had been obscured. What was formerly a flat, manicured plot of land was now a bumpy mass of mud and weeds. Even the solid, sturdy, iron railings that fenced half the graveyard perimeter were rusted and weather-beaten out of shape.

The dark, brooding place had long since become a fearful place for children and a source of their horror stories. Now many grieving families preferred to lay the remains of their loved ones in the more attractive, well-maintained plots of a neighbouring new town cemetery. There had not been a burial on the church grounds for over a year.

Such a state of affairs was unacceptable to Annabelle. After consultations with her parish council and the wider village, the reverend put her plan for revitalising the graveyard to a vote. With a new sense of purpose and the villager's somewhat tepid approval, Annabelle was filled with enthusiasm as she prepared for yet another invigorating project. Until she saw the costs.

Fixing a graveyard was a task far too detailed and delicate for mere elbow grease, some hearty volunteers, and a few shovels. Annabelle would need the deftest of green fingers to bring its wretched soil back to a state of well-nourished uniformity and the experience of a true craftsman to restore gravestones in such a bad state. She pulled a notepad and pencil from her cassock pocket and studied the figures again, the wind tossing her hair against her brow as vigorously as her thoughts rushed about her mind.

"If staring at the price made things cheaper," came a warm, lively voice from behind her, "then I'd have a house on the south coast of Spain already. Tea, Vicar?"

Annabelle spun around to see the familiar sight of her friend and church bookkeeper, Philippa, carefully threading her way between the stones. She held a mug of steaming tea in her hand.

"Oh yes, that's just what I need." Annabelle put her notepad away and took the cup.

"You'll catch your death of cold if you keep coming out here, Vicar. Why, you're not even wearing anything warm!"

Annabelle sipped slowly from her mug and gazed at the cemetery before musing, almost to herself, "We shall need another fundraiser."

"Reverend!" Philippa gasped as she hugged herself tightly against the wind. "We've already had *three* in the past month! The bake sale, the children's talent show, and the raffle. That raffle prize was one of the best I've ever seen! *A custom-made coat from Mrs. Shoreditch!* I've never seen such tailoring. I bought a dozen tickets myself!"

"Then why are we still so short?" Annabelle replied with a tone of exasperation that Philippa knew not to take personally. "We raised more money when we held a flower sale for the path to be re-gravelled! I just don't understand it."

Philippa sighed and placed a hand on the tall vicar's shoulder. Annabelle turned, her face a mixture of confusion and desperation.

"Are people tired of the church, Philippa?" Annabelle asked her. "Have they run out of sympathy for its causes? Maybe it's the graveyard. Perhaps it's too macabre for most of them to care about. Do they believe the childish tales of ghosts and goblins?"

As Annabelle gazed at her, Philippa opened her mouth as if to say something, before quickly closing it and putting a finger over her lips. "What?" Annabelle said, picking up on Philippa's hesitation. "What is it?"

With an unconvincing sigh, Philippa spoke quietly, as if someone nearby might hear. "Now Vicar, you know I hate nothing more than gossip and rumour-mongering. If I have one sin, it's that I'm harshly judgemental of those who engage in it . . ."

"Go on," Annabelle urged, stemming the impulse to roll her eyes. Philippa's skills in ferreting out village tittle-tattle were legendary.

Philippa sighed again. She looked around her carefully, her gesture adding weight to her words. "This is probably just idle speculation, of the kind dull types use to sound more intriguing, and bored types use to fill the time—"

"Come on, Philippa! At this rate, by the time you tell me your thoughts, I really will have caught a cold!"

"Well," Philippa said, unaffected by Annabelle's impatience, "I've heard it muttered in certain circles that many families are having financial difficulties."

Annabelle sipped her tea and frowned. "Doesn't every

family have financial difficulties at this time of year? So soon after taking expensive summer holidays, when the heating bills start coming in, and Christmas is just around the corner?"

"Perhaps, Reverend," Philippa said, her tone still conspiratorial and low, "but there's an added element here. You see, a lot of the women are complaining that their husbands are being stingy with money, hiding it. And they're saying the men are spending more and more time away from home."

Annabelle took another sip and frowned again. "But is that really anything new, Philippa? The football season is in full swing, and it's too cold to do anything but go to the pub in the evening."

Philippa closed her eyes and gave a brief shake of her head, annoyed that her privileged, secretive insights had been dismissed. "Perhaps, Reverend," she said, in a tightly-controlled tone, "but I just thought you'd like to know what your parishioners are saying."

"I'm sorry, Philippa. You're right. Maybe there is something to it. But financial difficulties or not, the result is the same." Annabelle turned back to face the gravestones. "Without help, this cemetery will remain a sorry state of affairs. If it snows again this year, I daren't think how much worse it could get."

"I'm sorry, Reverend. I'm sure we'll get it fixed," Philippa said, placing her hand on the vicar's arm again.

"Thank you for being so positive," Annabelle said, covering Philippa's hand with her own. "You know, I've taken to coming out here and praying. Even though it's cold and rather ugly, I've always felt like saying my prayers in places that need them most." Annabelle smiled. "I know it's terribly superstitious and silly for a vicar, but I even find myself looking for a sign. Some sort of signal from the Lord that'll help guide me."

Just then, a low, powerful, rumbling sound rolled through the air like a wave. Philippa and Annabelle clutched each other in shock.

"What was that?" Philippa squealed.

"I don't know!"

"Did you hear it?"

"Of course I heard it! I wouldn't be grabbing you if I hadn't!"

Another low hum reached them, louder and more melodic this time. The two women turned to face each other, their eyes wide, their mouths open. Then Annabelle chuckled. More notes were added to the riff, and the throbbing sound turned into a moving, atmospheric melody; the distinctive sound of the church organ.

"It's only Jeremy!" Annabelle said as Philippa let go of her arm, her blood pressure returning to normal.

"So it is," Philippa said, smiling. "He scared me half to death! It's rather early for him, though, isn't it? He doesn't usually start practicing until ten, and it's only eight."

Annabelle handed her empty cup to Philippa before straightening her clerical robe. "I'll see what he's up to. You'd better go feed those pups before they start digging up this graveyard for bones."

"Right you are, Vicar," Philippa said, turning away and leading Annabelle out of the graveyard.

"Did Janet give you any word on whether the shelter will be able to house them soon?"

"Not yet," Philippa replied. "I shall have a word with her today though, I imagine."

"No rush, I rather like having them around. Dogs are

such happy creatures. I think of them as a blessing, turning up out of the blue like that."

"Considering the state of them when they were found, huddled around their mother in the freezing cold, whining like human babies, I think they're the ones who feel blessed right now," Philippa responded.

The two women smiled at each other as they went their separate ways—Philippa to the cottage and its two wet-nosed house guests, Annabelle to the church, and her early-rising organ master.

CHAPTER TWO

"JEREMY!" ANNABELLE CALLED over the cascade of notes. "Jeremy! Yoo-hoo!"

It was only when Annabelle was close enough to energetically wave in Jeremy's peripheral vision that he stopped playing, so deeply was he engrossed in his music. He noticed her with a start and abruptly pulled his hands from the keyboard.

"Oh! Sorry, Vicar, I didn't see you there," he said, in his soft voice.

Jeremy Cunningham was an extremely tall, slim man, his rather pasty face topped with neatly-thatched blond hair. His pale complexion, blue eyes, and thin, pink lips betrayed his youthfulness but his penchant for thickly-knitted sweaters and sharply-creased trousers indicated a taste much older than his twenty-eight years.

"Don't apologise," Annabelle said, "it's rather lovely if a little macabre at this time of the morning."

"It's Brahm's *Requiem*. One of my favourites. I tend to play slower pieces in the morning to warm up my hands," he said, holding his fingers up and wiggling them with a polite smile.

"Indeed," Annabelle replied, marvelling at what she saw in front of her. "I must say, I continue to be amazed by the size of your hands, Jeremy. I've never seen such long, elegant fingers! They are quite extraordinary."

Jeremy nodded gracefully. "My old vicar in Bristol said that 'the Lord provides the very gifts we require to worship Him.'"

Annabelle smiled. Jeremy was one of the most devout members of her flock and one of the most recent additions. He had moved to Upton St. Mary six months ago and made Annabelle's acquaintance very quickly, presenting himself at the first opportunity to offer his services. She quickly found a use for him as the church organist. Jeremy immediately set to work cleaning and repairing the vintage organ. It was a complex contraption, with pipes that reached up one side of the stained glass window on the church's north wall, but Jeremy was up to the job.

Until the dexterous young man arrived in the village, the organ had stood dormant since the death of the previous church organist in 1989. Few members of Annabelle's parish even knew the pipes were there until they blasted into life one Sunday morning. It caused quite a stir. Postmistress Mrs. Turner nearly fainted, and Mr. Briggs, the local baker, thought he was having another heart attack. They both had to be attended by paramedic Joe Tucker as Annabelle hovered close by, mentally making a note to raise the idea of a defibrillator at the next parish council meeting.

Since then, Jeremy had taken it upon himself to keep the pipes sparkling clean. They often shimmered in the early morning glow that poured forth through the church's colourful windows. Jeremy also kept the keys dusted, the pedals oiled, and the wood that encased it all, well-polished.

His accompaniments to the hymns and other musical arrangements were an instant success, adding yet another quality to Annabelle's already popular services. The villagers quickly found themselves drawn to the shy, quiet, young man with nimble fingers who blossomed when the conversation turned to the Bible. Some of the more excitable ladies of the village had even taken it upon themselves to find the bachelor a nice young woman to meet.

For now, though, Jeremy was living with his grandmother, a pleasant woman in her nineties who lived alone in the village. Her health had recently taken a turn for the worse, and the support of her neighbours was no longer enough to ensure her well-being. Jeremy had left his position as a music teacher in Bristol to care for her during what many felt would be her last stretch on earth.

"It's rather early even for you, isn't it?" Annabelle inquired.

"I do apologise, Vicar. I would have looked for you, but I saw the door to the church was open and thought it best not to disturb you if I could—though I obviously did!"

"Oh no, not at all!" Annabelle chuckled. "You just startled us. Philippa and I were standing in the cemetery when you began. Not the sort of place you suddenly want to hear a requiem. I thought the dead were about to rise up!"

Jeremy's expression darkened. "Nobody but the Lord is capable of such a thing, Vicar, as you well know," he said in a clipped monotone.

Annabelle's chuckle was quickly replaced with a solemn, serious look. If there had been one deficit in their otherwise easy relationship, it was Jeremy's distinct lack of humour—particularly regarding matters of faith.

"Of course," Annabelle said in her most sanctimonious voice. "Well . . . carry on." Jeremy turned back to the organ as Annabelle spun on her heel and walked briskly away, her cheeks flushed.

Annabelle's discomfort was quickly dispelled when she walked out of the church and saw Philippa leaving her cottage with two bounding puppies at her heels. Their faces, with their black noses and big brown eyes, were framed by pairs of floppy ears that flapped constantly. Both tan in colour, the female of the two was distinguished by a white streak that ran from the top of her head to the tip of her nose. As soon as they heard Annabelle's feet on the gravel, they ran to greet her.

"*Hello!*" Annabelle cooed cheerily, crouching down to scrub their ears. They yipped and panted their approval. She looked up at Philippa. "Are you taking them to Janet?"

"Yes," Philippa said, taking the opportunity to attach their leads whilst Annabelle distracted them. "For a check-up and a chat. Are you *sure* you want me to give them to the shelter?"

Annabelle pursed her lips as she stroked the soft fur of the floppy-eared strays. "Oh, I don't know, Philippa. It's a big responsibility. We would have to buy all sorts of things for them, and what about the flowers? Once they get bigger, they might trample all over the garden!"

"Hmm, they haven't done it yet. They've actually been rather well-behaved for a couple of puppies."

"They certainly have," Annabelle said, giving them one more playful chuck behind the ears before standing up. "But dogs are like people—they can do the most unexpected things."

Philippa smiled. "But you do say that we must help our

fellow man when he is in need. I'm sure that applies to dogs too."

"We've already got Biscuit."

"Oh! That cat's never around! Anyway, she's already taken a shine to them. You should have seen them all sleeping together this morning."

"You seem awfully fond of them. Why don't you adopt them?"

"I would, Reverend, but I spend so much time at the church that they might as well live here all the time." She looked down at the two puppies standing to attention, their tails wagging, their big brown eyes fixed on Annabelle. "Plus, they seem to have made their own preference rather clear."

"We'll see," said Annabelle. She headed to the cottage.

CHAPTER THREE

IT WAS STILL early when Annabelle got into her Mini Cooper later that morning. She did so with the same satisfaction she had felt on the day she bought it. She settled herself snugly into the seat, pulled her seatbelt across her chest, and turned the keys in the ignition. The motor chugged into life, and Annabelle felt a sense of girlish delight emanate from her hands on the wheel. As long as she could drive her little Mini wherever she liked, she would be happy; a simple but endless pleasure.

The car had always been more than a mere mode of transport for the reverend. As she spent most of her days either in church or around others, she appreciated the opportunity to enjoy the idyllic landscape. The beauty of the small Cornish village and the local countryside had been one of the most compelling reasons behind her decision to leave her inaugural clerical position in London. A decision she had not regretted.

Now winter was upon them, the cold weather made it difficult to take the kinds of jaunts across endless fields and through sun-speckled woods that she enjoyed so much in the summertime. And so the satisfaction of being cocooned in the Mini's small yet cosy interior whilst the fields and hedgerows sped by her was never greater. With the Mini's tiny heater on full blast and its puppy-esque enthusiasm for the open road, she never felt uncomfortable or confined inside it.

Annabelle had built up a warm affection for the Mini, which she lovingly kept pristine. In her more whimsical moods, she even fancied that it spoke to her. The easy thrum of its engine signalled the contentment of a cat's purr, whilst the gentle squeak of a seat as she sat on it was like a greeting from an old friend. Even the bumps and wheezes of the car's suspension as it navigated obstacles in the road sounded like the grunts and groans of an old man getting up from an armchair.

The musical tics and idiosyncrasies of her Mini were like a song Annabelle knew intimately, which is why she found herself increasingly bothered by the weak sound of the engine as she drove to the hamlet at Folly's Bottom. She intended to discuss the failing attempts to raise funds for the cemetery renovations with a parish council member there, but she barely reached the halfway point of the five-mile trip when the Mini Cooper's trials grew noticeably worse.

"What on earth is the matter with you?" Annabelle pressed the accelerator harder and found the Mini struggling to respond with its typical ready increase in speed.

For the next half-mile, the Mini's engine alternately faltered and hummed, occasionally sputtering back into life with a snap, only to trail off once more. Eventually, Annabelle's fear became a reality—the car stopped entirely.

Annabelle turned the key back and forth a few times in an attempt to get the car started, but the Mini only offered a limp whine in response. Taking deep breaths, Annabelle refused to get angry. Instead, she lifted her gaze to the car's roof and silently demanded an explanation from God.

Tightening her coat around her, she stepped out into the chilly wind and closed the door. For a brief moment, she considered checking beneath the bonnet for the cause of the car's problems, but she quickly realised that would be of little use. Annabelle's passion for her car did not extend to an interest in anything mechanical, and she didn't want to make anything worse. She looked in both directions up and down the road, and with one final huff and a frown, she began to walk back to Upton St. Mary. She'd have to visit the local garage.

A short way into her trek, Annabelle decided to take a shortcut to avoid a large curve in the road. She took a small, rough path, fenced on both sides by hedgerows, fields, and hills. For a few minutes, Annabelle was rather pleased with herself. She felt proud of her knowledge of the extensive web of footpaths, lanes, and farm tracks that radiated from, through, and around Upton St. Mary. Her sense of triumph proved brief, however, when soon into her walk she found the entire way ahead obstructed by a densely packed herd of cows. They were traipsing slowly to their milking shed.

"Excuse me!" Annabelle politely asked as she tottered behind, nudging the cows to find a gap. "Vicar coming through!"

She quickly realised the animals were—rather rudely, in her opinion—in no mood to let her pass, their stoic faces uninterested in her pleas, their large bodies incapable of moving at greater speed. Annabelle gazed beyond the large mass of white, brown, and black to find farmer Leo Tremethick at their head.

"Leo! Over here! Leo!" she called, waving her arms frantically like a woman drowning at sea.

The overall-clad figure in the distance briefly turned and removed his flat cap to wave at the reverend. Annabelle smiled broadly at him, thinking the farmer would surely do something to allow her to pass. Instead, he merely smiled back, gestured at the cows, and shrugged his shoulders. The meaning was clear; there was nothing he could do. He shouted something that Annabelle couldn't quite make out over the sound of cows mooing, then turned back to trudge on in front of them.

"I know that your cows are God's creatures," Annabelle exclaimed, as she narrowly avoided being splattered by yet another cowpat, "but I really must say, you're showing very little respect for the authority of the church!"

For a full twelve minutes, Annabelle inched along the muddy, manure-filled path behind the herd, encouraged only by the prospect of treating herself to a nice slice of cake when she reached her journey's end. When the cows finally turned off the path to stroll into their milking shed, she hurried forwards to the junction where the path rejoined the road. Her shortcut had taken longer than if she had stuck to the pretty country lane. It would have been less cowpat-strewn too.

Annabelle continued on her way to the garage. It was situated on the outskirts of the village, across the road from one of its largest pubs. The lanes were mostly empty of traffic, but at one point, she was buffeted by a speeding black, sporty Mercedes Benz with dark tinted windows. It was the kind of car one would usually encounter outside a nightclub in a bustling city. It stood out in this bucolic part of the country.

The villagers of Upton St. Mary, and indeed, the

wealthier families who lived on the estates surrounding the village, had rather conservative tastes in cars. SUVs, the odd BMW, possibly a classic British sports car, or a luxury sedan were the most expensive vehicles that one was likely to find on the local roads. Most people drove pickup trucks, small hatchbacks, or minivans. The very notion of blacked-out windows seemed preposterous. Annabelle wondered who could possibly be driving such a car, or even more intriguingly, why on earth did they feel the need to hide away. She frowned as she watched the car disappear into the distance. It had been an uncommon morning so far.

CHAPTER FOUR

ANNABELLE'S RUMINATIONS WERE quickly interrupted when a small van pulled up beside her. She immediately recognised it and walked up to the window.

"Alfred Roper!" Annabelle exclaimed. "How are you? Off to a job?"

"Aye, Vicar. Busy weekend."

Alfred had become well-known for his gardening and landscaping skills during the thirty-odd years he had been tending to the grounds of larger houses in the area. He was almost sixty, yet the fresh air and physical nature of his work gave him a fit, powerful bearing. His brown eyes and grizzled beard were rarely accompanied by anything other than a pleasant smile, and Annabelle always enjoyed his company.

"But not too busy that I can't give you a lift," he continued with a wink. "Hop in." Annabelle clapped her hands and eagerly got inside the earthy-smelling van, its comforting warmth making her realise how cold she was.

"Thank you so much, Alfred. My car—"

"Broke down on the road to Folly's Bottom? Aye, I just passed it," Alfred said in his gruff voice.

"Yes." Annabelle laughed. "If you could just drop me off—"

"At Mildred's Garage? Of course, Vicar." Annabelle smiled and settled into her seat.

"Well, I owe you a cup of tea for this at the very least, Alfred. Do drop by the church when you find the time."

"Oh, it's nothing, Vicar. I always offer. You're the fourth person I've picked up from the side of the road this week."

Annabelle looked at Alfred in disbelief. "Really?" she said.

"Aye, if you ask me, it's all these new *technologies* they keep sticking in the cars. So many dongles and apps and mp3s and i-whatsits—something's bound to go wrong! I don't even trust automatic transmissions myself," he said, patting his gearstick affectionately.

"But Alfred, my car is a Mini! It might have go-faster stripes, but it's hardly tricked out with all the latest doodads, for heaven's sake!"

Alfred shrugged before lifting his chin. "Probably the spark plugs then. Yeah. That'll be it."

Alfred pulled the van over to the kerb in front of Mildred's Garage. He nodded politely as Annabelle effusively offered her gratitude and repeated her promise of a cup of tea. She waved as he sped off to his next job and walked over to the low, wide building that housed the garage's workshop.

The garage had seen better days. Its paint was peeling, and the large metal shutters that fronted the workshop were rusty. But the reputation of the business was spotless. Since inheriting the garage from her father nearly thirty-five years earlier, long-time Upton St. Mary resident Mildred Smith had overseen the purchases and maintenance of most of the villager's very first cars, their upgrades to family vehicles, and, for the more successful community members, their luxury vehicles and sports cars. In many respects, Annabelle often thought she and Mildred were much alike, both witnessing and supporting people through the gravest and grandest milestones of their lives.

Though the world had changed and most vehicles were now, as Alfred had said, computers on wheels, Mildred's was still a comforting first port of call for many when a knocking started, a tire ran flat, or a simple oil change was needed. In many respects, much of the garage's popularity was down to its old-fashioned values. People knew they would get a job well done for a fair price at Mildred's—and more often than not, with plenty of courtesy and a cup of tea thrown in. She or her mechanics would even pump petrol whilst drivers sat in the comfort of their cars, a luxury long since abandoned just about everywhere else in England.

Annabelle marched across the forecourt, in between the vintage cars, restoration projects Mildred enjoyed in her spare time. She scanned the garage for a glimpse of Mildred's frizzy, red hair. Despite being sixty-two, Mildred was enthusiastic, gnarly, and as strong as an ox—though only half the size.

"Mildred!" she called. "Mildred! It's Annabelle!"

Annabelle noticed the peculiar silence that permeated the garage. She visited at least once a week to fuel up and got regular check-ups for her car throughout the year. But she had never seen it as quiet as this. It often seemed that

Mildred spent every waking hour at the garage, hammering or clanking away at some problem or dealing with the phone calls that seemed to interrupt her work every few minutes. On the rare occasions that Mildred was away, one of her assistants would be there: Ted, a grizzled man in his forties who always wore the pained, despondent expression of a man recovering from a hangover, or Aziz, the teenage apprentice who would, to the chagrin of his colleagues, blare hip hop music from a device on his workbench as he tinkered with the cars.

One of the workshop's bays was occupied, a small hatchback neatly parked. Annabelle stepped inside, around the hatchback, and alongside the cluttered workbench.

"Ted! Aziz! Anyone?"

Annabelle knew Mildred well enough to know that neither she nor her assistants would leave the garage unattended, not without a notice of some kind. Something was severely amiss. She walked around spinning as she scanned the workshop walls and the two bays.

Apart from the hatchback, there was no other vehicle inside, and with the garage's open plan, there were few nooks and crannies to investigate. Annabelle paced anxiously, studying everything around her for something out of the ordinary.

Just as she was about to go outside in search of clues, she crouched and looked beneath the small car in the middle of the workshop. It was dark, the lights of the pit beneath the car were off. Annabelle strained to remember what such pits looked like. At the far end, she noticed something sticking out. A tool of some kind. She stood up, walked to the other end, and crouched once more to see what it was and whether it might illuminate the mystery of the empty garage.

"Oh dear God!" Annabelle suddenly squealed, pulling back and covering her mouth. She had been mistaken.

What she had seen rising from the pit was no tool.

It was nothing mechanical of any kind.

It was a hand.

CHAPTER FIVE

ANNABELLE FORCED HERSELF to crouch again. She could see the hand reaching out from the pit, imploring. After squinting and shuffling to gain a better look, Annabelle was in no doubt that the hand's rough texture and slim, taut muscles could only belong to one person—Mildred.

"Mildred!" Annabelle called desperately. "Mildred, are you alright?" The hand remained still.

Annabelle stood and looked around nervously. She considered her options. She could seek out the car keys and move the hatchback, but there was no guarantee she would find them, and she would waste precious, possibly crucial time trying. She could call 999 but she patted herself down in search of her phone without success. She stamped her foot when she realised she had left it on her Mini's dashboard. She considered using the garage phone to call for help before reconsidering. Something troubling had happened here, and that phone might prove an important clue. Annabelle had seen enough drama as a priest to know how important it was to leave a scene intact.

There was only one option. Annabelle launched herself from the garage with long, powerful strides. The Silver Swan. The pub across the road. *I'll get help there—maybe it won't be too late.*

Upton St. Mary boasted three pubs, the Dog and Duck, the King's Head, and the Silver Swan. To outsiders, it might seem a tad excessive for a small village to have three drinking establishments, but it is by no means unusual in England. Annabelle had been inside all of them on one occasion or another. The Silver Swan was a rather different pub from the other two. The Dog and Duck and the King's Head had catered to the working men of Upton St. Mary for generations, the air above their mahogany tables always filled with the forceful thrust of male conversation. Meanwhile the Silver Swan attracted a decidedly more diverse clientele.

The Silver Swan had been owned and managed by the same family for three generations. With its hearty meals, leather chairs, and large fireplace, no patron left without feeling as if they had been a welcome visitor in someone's home rather than a mere consumer of their excellent local beer. Pub-goers at the Dog and Duck and Kings Head could play a game of darts or pool and drink the stoutest ales, but the Silver Swan had a large outside seating area. This alone made it a beacon for all the outdoor adventurers who enjoyed the miles of gorgeous countryside surrounding Upton St. Mary.

Every day, hikers would plan their routes so they arrived at the pub at lunchtime. Every Saturday and Sunday, the local cycling club began and ended their scenic rural rides there. Until they were banned, the local pipe-smoking club convened to puff away at the outdoor benches whilst comparing tobaccos. Yes, it was a place that did brisk business, indeed.

Inevitably, the weekends were always busiest for The Silver Swan. Families came together to enjoy its Sunday roasts and welcoming atmosphere. Even at this early hour, half the tables were filled with families chattering through their breakfasts when Annabelle, panting and looking wildly about, burst through its large doors.

She made a beeline for the bar, already preparing to explain the situation to the barman in the most efficient manner. She didn't want to waste any time. But she stopped suddenly, catching sight of someone familiar in the corner of her eye. The tall, imposing—and somewhat dashing, she had to admit—figure of Detective Inspector Mike Nicholls sat alone at a table. The exact man she might have hoped to bump into at this particular moment.

Changing direction, she weaved through the tables to his booth, where he was engrossed in the study of a large map. She slapped her palms on the table. He looked up with the kind of seasoned expression you would expect from an officer of the law who had dealt with agitated members of the public many times before.

"Inspector! What are you doing here?"

"Hello, Reverend," he replied. He was relaxed despite Annabelle's aggressive approach. "I'm glad I bumped into you. You wouldn't happen to know where I could find a James Paynton around here by any—"

"Never mind that," Annabelle interrupted breathlessly. "Something very serious has happened to Mildred!"

"Mildred?"

"The mechanic who owns the garage across the road."

The inspector raised an eyebrow. "What's happened?"

"It would be easier to show you, Inspector. You'd better call an ambulance."

The inspector was more accustomed to giving orders than taking them, particularly from officious vicars. However, the look of shock on Annabelle's pale face, as well as the grudging trust he had developed in her during their partnership solving two recent crimes, made him scrunch up his map and follow her hastily out of the pub.

As they jogged across the road, the inspector called an ambulance and some police backup for good measure. They reached the garage, and Annabelle led him to the pit. The two of them bent down as she pointed out what was now unmistakably Mildred's hand—it hadn't moved.

"We'd better shift the car," Nicholls said, standing up.

"The keys might be in the office," Annabelle said. She felt more confident now that she was in the presence of a policeman. They stood in the doorway of the tiny office, rapidly scanning the mass of paperwork and files that filled the desk and shelves.

"Those must be the keys," Nicholls said finally, pointing to a set marked with a Ford emblem hanging on the wall next to where Annabelle stood. She spun around and picked them off the hook.

"Why don't you move the car?" the inspector said.

Annabelle nodded self-importantly and darted to the vehicle, followed by the now-thoughtful inspector. Annabelle got in the car, started the ignition, and reversed out of the garage, throwing daylight onto the pit and its contents. When she returned to the workshop, Nicholls was crouching again, scrutinising the pit. He put his hand up.

"You may not want to see this, Reverend," he cautioned.

The warning only made Annabelle more curious, and she quickly moved to the inspector's side.

"Oh!" she said, her voice fluttering with shock.

There lay Mildred and, there was no doubt about it, she was dead. Her body leant face-first against the side of the pit, one arm extended upwards, her hand poised in mid-air like she was waving. Her other arm lay by her side. Her overalls bore the marks of numerous fluids, but there was no mistaking the dark-red stain that trailed from her skull onto her collar. The back of her ever-wild, red hair was matted with blood. The inspector sighed, stood up, and walked away.

"Where are you going?" Annabelle said, her voice quivering with fear and grief.

"To call off the ambulance," the inspector replied, pulling his phone from his coat pocket. "We need a pathologist and scenes of crime officers."

CHAPTER SIX

IN LESS THAN an hour, the once-silent garage became a hotbed of activity. Over a dozen officers were combing the entire area for evidence, the crackle of their radios filling the air. Over the noise of the officers, the commanding voice of pathologist, Harper Jones, could easily be heard as she directed her crew in the tricky task of extracting the body from its most unlikely of graves.

Annabelle clutched herself tightly as she stood in front of the open garage, her shivering only partly due to the cold. She had, of course, seen a lot of death in her line of work, yet rarely as the result of murder.

Annabelle felt tremendously sad. She had always shared a strong bond with Mildred. The car mechanic and businesswoman had been a pillar of the community, a friend to everyone who passed through her garage, and a role model for all. Annabelle knew for certain that the sense of shock she was now feeling was only the beginning of a wave that would affect the entire village. Mildred had been a woman who had served the community of Upton St. Mary for decades, and Annabelle had developed a tremendous amount of respect and admiration for her. A beneficiary of Mildred's work and generosity, Annabelle had often thought that if she was half as good at her job, she would be very proud indeed.

"Are you okay, Reverend?" the inspector asked her. Annabelle felt his broad, comforting hand on her shoulder.

She turned to face him and forced a weak smile. "I should be used to this," she said, "considering what I do."

"Nobody gets used to losing people," Nicholls said in a low voice. "I take it you knew her well?"

"Quite well. As did most of the villagers."

Nicholls turned to gaze at the activity inside the garage before turning back to her. "Reverend, you know I'll have to ask you a few questions."

"Of course."

"But if you're still in shock, I can give you some time to compose yourself. Leave it until evening, perhaps. I shouldn't really, it's against procedure, but . . . well . . . it's you. If I can't bend a few rules, then I may as well be a constable."

Annabelle smiled at the inspector's clumsy effort at humour. "Thank you very much, Inspector. But I assure you, I'm fine. If anything, the sadness makes me even more willing to do anything I can to help."

Returning her smile, Nicholls reached into his pocket to fish out his notebook. "When did you find Mildred?"

"Minutes before I met you, Inspector. My car had broken down on the road to Folly's Bottom. I walked for a whilst until Alfred Roper came along and offered me a lift. As soon as I entered the garage, I noticed how . . . *quiet* everything was. I called out to see if Mildred or her mechanics were here, but there was no reply. I was about to leave when it occurred to me to look under the car. That's when I saw the . . . hand." Her voice broke on the last word.

Inspector Nicholls pulled a packet of tissues from his pocket. He offered it to Annabelle. She blew her nose loudly.

"Thank you, Inspector," she said, a little more composed.

"You said something about Mildred's mechanics?"

"Yes. Ted and Aziz."

"Can you tell me anything about them?"

"Let's see . . . Ted Lovesey. He's in his forties. He's worked here since I arrived in Upton St. Mary three years ago. He's a rather pleasant man if a little . . . *indulgent*."

"What do you mean by that?" Nicholls asked.

"Well, he smokes heavily, drinks heavily. Has a rather keen eye for the ladies and tends to lose his money as quickly as he earns it. But other than that, he's a wonderful member of our community."

"Any idea where he is now?"

"Oh, still recovering from his Friday night, I shouldn't wonder. He lives alone on Violet Lane."

Nicholls scribbled on his notepad. "And this . . . Aziz?"

Annabelle pondered for a moment before answering. "Aziz Malik is his full name. Actually, he should be here today. He's a teenager and works at the weekends and some evenings."

"Okay, I'll follow up with him. Can you tell me a little about Mildred?"

"She was the nicest person you could possibly imagine. She lived nearby but she spent almost all her time at the garage. She never really spoke about family or relationships, but I understand she never married and had no siblings.

The only relative she had that I heard of was her father, and he passed away over thirty years ago."

"So you can't think of any reason why someone would do this to her? Possible grudges? Maybe a high repair bill? A poor job?"

"Absolutely not!" Annabelle said, horrified at the thought. "She was loved by everyone! Her prices were very fair—if not overly so! And as for her workmanship Mildred could turn a rust bucket into a rocket ship quicker than one could say thank you!"

The inspector tapped his pencil against his lips as he considered what she said. "Perhaps she was too good."

"What do you mean?"

"Well, if I owned a garage, and I had to compete with someone spoken of with the level of enthusiasm you use when talking about Mildred, I'd feel pretty resentful."

Annabelle frowned. "But . . . there *is* no competition. Mildred's Garage is the only one in Upton St. Mary."

Nicholls snorted. "There's *always* competition, Reverend. Even when it seems otherwise."

"Who?"

"Well, you say your car has broken down. It seems unlikely you'll be able to use this garage to fix it—so who will you go to now?"

Annabelle's eyes widened. "Crawford Motors. In Crenoweth, it's about ten miles away. It's run by Ian Crawford. But I'm sure he's not behi—"

"Why not? How well do you know him?"

Annabelle stuttered as she sought the right words, somehow feeling she was condemning someone without proof. "Well . . . not very well. I've only used his garage a few times."

Inspector Nicholls scribbled in his notebook. "I know

you prefer to see the good in people, Reverend, but it's my job to see the bad. And this guy sounds like a possible suspect to my ears."

"Inspector. Reverend." A cool, calm voice interrupted them.

Annabelle and the inspector immediately turned to see Harper Jones walking towards them. Dr. Jones had been the local pathologist for more than a few years now. She possessed a gritty determination that showed little sign of abating. With her raven-black hair and sharp features, her striking looks brought her attention wherever she went but only those who knew the extent of her talent truly saw how remarkable she was.

"What have you got for me, Harper?" the inspector said, knowing that the pathologist preferred to avoid small talk.

"She was killed in the pit. Blunt force to the back of the head. My early assessment is that there were multiple strikes. Quick. Rapid. The weapon must have been long enough to swing hard, and heavy enough to strike deep. The garage and pit are full of such objects, could have been any of them. There's a lot of blood confusing things too along with plenty of other fluids—petrol, oil, lubricants. It's a mess. My guys are taking the body away now, as well as the tools. We'll study them and hopefully find which one was the murder weapon. After that, I'll pass it on to your people for fingerprinting."

It was a brutal summation. Harper Jones didn't mess around.

CHAPTER SEVEN

THE INSPECTOR LOOKED at Annabelle, concerned that she would be affected by Harper's recounting of the gruesome details of Mildred's death. He needn't have worried. If anything, Annabelle's focus on the facts was almost as intense as the pathologist's.

"She was killed *inside* the pit?" Annabelle asked quickly. Harper looked at Annabelle and nodded.

"But, the car..." Annabelle said.

"She was definitely murdered in the pit," Harper confirmed. "There'd be blood everywhere if she was killed outside it."

"Was she already in the pit when she was attacked, or could she have been dragged into the pit, and then killed?" Annabelle asked.

"Either is a possibility," Harper said, her blunt tone mellowing. "We should check the floor for signs that she was dragged, but there aren't any signs of a struggle."

"Can anyone get in and out of that pit when there's a car over it?" the inspector asked.

"Mildred could," Annabelle replied. "She was rather

slight. Even if the car was small and low to the ground like my Mini, she could climb down quite easily."

"What about Ted? Or the teenager?"

"Certainly not Ted. His paunch wouldn't allow it. Aziz probably could," Annabelle said, before suddenly feeling that she was incriminating someone again.

"Hmm," the inspector said, tapping his pencil against his pad. "That leaves us with two options. Either somebody small—possibly Aziz—slid into the pit whilst Mildred was working and killed her, or someone threw her in there, killed her, then parked the car over the top."

"And put the keys back on the rack of the office wall," Annabelle added, her voice softening at the thought of such cold-blooded behaviour. "Maybe we should check them for fingerprints?"

"Cars and their keys are some of the worst things to get fingerprints from," Harper said. "Too many people handle them. You did, remember. I've checked the car for traces of blood, and the keys for fingerprints, but I've not found anything. Whoever did this was very careful."

"Cauldwell!" Nicholls spoke sharply to a nearby officer.

"Yes, Inspector?" An eager young man responded, appearing quickly by his side.

"It's a long shot, but I want to know who that hatchback belongs to and why it was in the garage." The inspector tore a sheet from his pad and handed it to the constable. "Another thing, Aziz Malik and Ted Lovesey. Find them and bring them in for questioning."

"Yes, sir!" The young officer left. Nicholls turned to Harper.

"Thanks, Harper. Keep me posted."

The pathologist nodded curtly before returning to the crime scene, leaving Annabelle and the inspector standing outside on the garage forecourt. They looked at each other awkwardly until Annabelle broke the silence.

"I must say, today has been full of strange occurrences."

"Has it?"

"It's been one thing after another."

"What do you mean?"

"Oh, it's nothing, really."

"Tell me, it could be important," the inspector insisted, his curiosity quickly turning professional.

"Where do I start!? I mean, it's nothing next to the fact that one of my dearest community members has just been murdered in cold blood."

"Still, your observations could be material to the case."

"The devil is in the details, I believe you mean," Annabelle said, smiling despite herself.

Nicholls chuckled. "I wouldn't use such words. Wouldn't want to offend you."

"Tosh!" Annabelle exclaimed. "I've far too much to worry about to be offended by things like that."

"Can I offer you a lift somewhere?" the inspector asked.

Annabelle smiled, shyly this time. "Back to my car would be most helpful, Inspector."

"Of course, Reverend." They began walking across the road to the Silver Swan, where the inspector's car was parked.

"So, about these 'strange' things . . ." he began.

"Ah yes, well, my Mini breaking down for one thing. Not that it's strange in itself, but it was the *way* that it happened. If I had to guess, and I can only guess because I know nothing worth knowing about cars, it was as if something wore out."

"These things happen."

"I know. But Mildred was really very good at spotting problems. And I only brought my car in last week."

"What for?"

"Oh, just to fuel it up."

"Well, she couldn't have diagnosed any problem from that. Not unless she checked the engine as well."

"But then there was a car I noticed earlier today. It was very odd, much flashier than anything you typically see around here—even those owned by the wealthier estate owners are more subdued."

"Hmm."

"It even had blacked-out windows. Imagine that!"

"Could have been a limo. Somebody important heading to the city."

Annabelle shook her head. "No. Unless it was owned by one of the very few families in Folly's Bottom, and I can certainly say it wasn't, it wouldn't have been going that way. There are much quicker routes to take."

"Are you thinking it could have something to do with what happened at the garage? Should I ask my boys to run some checks?"

As they walked, Annabelle looked at the inspector with a mischievous smile. "Inspector, are you asking for my advice concerning your investigation?"

Nicholls laughed easily. "You tend to offer it regardless."

Annabelle grinned. "No, I don't think so. The car was going so fast that it would have overshot the garage, and it wasn't long after that I got the ride from Alfred. There was no time to . . ." She trailed off, looking forlorn.

"It was probably a villager's more successful relative who'd come down from London," the inspector said quickly, keen to return to safer conversational ground.

"Perhaps." Annabelle rallied, but she remained unconvinced. "But then there was the rumour I heard this morning."

"Oh?" the inspector said.

"Some nonsense about the men of Upton St. Mary disappearing all night and spending lots of money."

"Ah," Nicholls said. "Well, that's only natural for this time of year. The football season's started, and those tickets aren't cheap. And it's too cold to do anything but go to the pub." Annabelle laughed quietly almost to herself.

"What?" the inspector asked. "Something I said?"

"No," Annabelle replied, "but that was my conclusion exactly."

They reached the inspector's car. Annabelle walked around to the passenger side. Nicholls opened his door, but before he could get in, Annabelle spoke to him over the roof.

"There was one more thing," she said.

The inspector looked at her. "What?"

"Something you said to me just before we left the Silver Swan. You asked me where you could find James Paynton."

Nicholls laughed nervously as if he'd been caught out. "That's one mystery you can almost certainly solve for me."

"Yes," Annabelle smiled, "but it poses another: Why are you visiting a pedigree dog breeder in Upton St. Mary?"

Nicholls stretched out his arm and checked his watch. "If you're not in a rush to get your car, maybe you can accompany me, and I'll tell you on the way. I was supposed to meet him half an hour ago."

CHAPTER EIGHT

"IS THIS NOT a strange time to be running errands, Inspector? You've only just discovered a dead body," Annabelle said as she settled herself into the passenger seat of the inspector's car. "Shouldn't you be investigating, um, something?"

"If I had to take a break, now is the best time. The boys are out looking for Mildred's mechanics, and Harper needs to conduct the post-mortem. I can't do much more right now."

"I see," Annabelle said.

"Anyway, thank you for helping, Reverend." The inspector put the car into gear and urged it into the road. "Today is going to be very busy, what with all this trouble. Any time saved is much appreciated."

"Please, think nothing of it, Inspector." Annabelle smiled before noticing the small screen perched in the middle of the inspector's dashboard. She pointed at it and looked at him with bewilderment. "But you've got a GPS? Won't that get you to Paynton's place?"

"That thing?" Nicholls said. "Never use it. Can't stand them. Give me a proper map any day."

Annabelle chuckled and leant towards him. "Something of a technophobe, are we? An old-fashioned man? These GPS's are really rather simple to use, you know, once you learn the ins and outs."

"Oh, I know how to use it alright," the inspector responded.

"Then why do you prefer a map? A GPS is so much easier and faster. And safer. You can't exactly open a map every few minutes whilst driving. Especially along these lanes. You need to keep your eye on the road."

Nicholls sighed as if his reasons were long, burdensome, and deeply held. "I don't like the GPS for exactly those reasons. It's easier and faster."

Annabelle furrowed her brow. She wondered if she had misheard him. "I'm not sure I follow."

"Reverend, my job depends on me having tightly-honed instincts. I need a sharp mind, keen eyes, and quick wits. But it's very difficult to maintain those when you have a hunk of plastic and a microchip doing most of your thinking for you. The brain gets lazy."

"Ah," Annabelle said, nodding her head. "I understand. Turn left here, by the way. James lives about a mile up this road."

The inspector followed her direction, then said, "What will you do about your car?"

"I shall call a tow truck. It should be alright. I steered it off the road when the engine stopped."

"Well, I'll happily drive you to it once I'm done with my appointment."

"Thank you," Annabelle said. There was a pause. "I

must say, I'm incredibly curious as to why you're visiting a dog breeder."

"Ah," the inspector said, remembering his promise to reveal all. "Well, my ex-wife got Lulu. My dog."

"Surely not!" Annabelle exclaimed. "You adored that dog!"

"I did." Nicholls sighed. "But so did my wife. Not as much as me, but enough. It was the only aspect of the divorce that we fought over."

"I'm sorry, Inspector."

Nicholls breathed in deeply. "It was inevitable. I'm a detective. It's a difficult job, and the hours can get very long. I had a neighbour who fed Lulu when I was stuck at work and a few regular dog walkers, but . . . it wasn't enough. Not for the judge at least. "

Annabelle remained silent as the inspector's voice trailed off. There wasn't much she could say, and she knew from experience that listening was often more appreciated than offering advice. After a few moments, James Paynton's vast property came into view, and Annabelle took the opportunity to distract the inspector from his thoughts.

"Here we are," she said, pointing at the buildings.

Beyond the immaculately maintained wooden fencing surrounding its large, bright green front lawn, the modern, two-storey, L-shaped farmhouse stood proudly at the end of a long driveway. As the inspector drove up, he took notice of his surroundings, judging from them how well-off the owners were.

The house was lush with decoration. Well-maintained, overflowing hanging baskets were arranged around an exquisitely carved front door. A large conservatory was attached to one side of the house, perfectly placed to receive just the right amount of light, even on the most overcast days. On the other side of the house were three paddocks containing five horses that looked, to the inspector's untrained eye, like thoroughbreds, their coats gleaming as they quietly grazed. Two Range Rovers with personalised number plates and a luxury convertible were parked next to a bank of stables to the rear. At the back of the farmhouse were two brick-built barns and no fewer than four pens of varying sizes. It was apparent even at a distance that an extraordinary amount of money was swashing about here and that even the most casual observer was to know it.

The inspector pulled up and parked between a classic Jaguar and a boat trailer. He turned the car engine off and looked around.

"Are you sure this is the place?"

"Of course, Inspector."

Nicholls whistled softly. "The dog business certainly pays better than the police force."

"Well, James's dogs are sought after by people from all over Britain —perhaps the world. They do very well in dog shows. His basset hounds are particularly popular."

"So I've heard."

"I take it you're here in search of a new dog?"

"That's the plan," he said, opening the door.

"Inspector! Wait!" Annabelle said, clutching his arm to stop him from getting out of the car. He turned around and looked at her hand in surprise. "I've just realised! Oh yes! It's almost too perfect!"

"What is?" Nicholls said, bemused.

"A few weeks ago, after morning tea, Philippa and I were inspecting the church grounds when we stumbled on a stray and her puppies amidst the undergrowth beside the cemetery. We immediately called Janet—she runs the local dog shelter—and asked for her help. Unfortunately, due to a mishap between a Doberman and a pit bull, she couldn't take all the pups, so Philippa and I decided to care for two of them until she's ready."

The inspector's face remained blank as if he was expecting more. "Well, that's a nice story. I hope things resolve themselves soon."

"But don't you *see*, Inspector? The timing is simply perfect! It's almost as if it were planned by the Lord himself!"

With growing exasperation, the inspector closed his car door and focused all his attention on Annabelle. "What are you trying to say, Reverend?"

"Why, that you should adopt the pups!"

"Oh, brother," Nicholls said, looking up and sighing. "One minute someone's taking away the only dog I have, the next I'm getting offered more dogs than I can handle."

"They're simply delightful little creatures, Inspector. Impossible not to love."

"What are they? Labs? German shepherds?"

"Well . . . They're, um, mixed."

"Mongrels."

"Yes, but they're extremely well-behaved. Energetic and full of beans, but they haven't destroyed anything important yet." Nicholls raised a suspicious eyebrow. "Nothing but an old cushion I never liked anyway," Annabelle added. She was getting flustered beneath his intense gaze. "A few items of clothing, maybe, but I had too many. Regardless, it's all just part of their charm. You really must see them, Inspector."

"Look, Reverend, ordinarily I'd jump at the chance to help you out and take one of them off your hands—"

"It's not for my sake, Inspector!" Annabelle exclaimed, her blush of embarrassment turning to one of exasperation.

"It's for *theirs!* These dogs need a home! The dog shelter is wonderful, but they deserve an owner who will love and respect them!"

"Don't these dogs need a home, too?" the inspector asked, gesturing towards the farmhouse.

Annabelle snorted. "These are pedigree dogs. They are bred to order. People pay hundreds of pounds for the privilege of giving them a home!"

Nicholls softened his gaze and breathed for a few moments, allowing the silence to take the edge off their terse conversation.

"Reverend. My job is very demanding," he said in a soft, persuading voice. "I need a dog that is disciplined, healthy, well-adjusted. I simply wouldn't be able to handle a stray."

"Hmph," Annabelle grumbled, folding her arms and looking out of the side window. "You know, I once read a rather apt saying: 'People who love dogs, love them all. People who love themselves will pick an expensive one.'"

Nicholl's looked at Annabelle quizzically. "I can't recall having heard that particular saying before."

Annabelle raised her chin and held his gaze. The inspector opened his mouth to say something but found himself at a loss for words. He shook his head and got out of the car. Annabelle pursed her lips, then quickly did the same.

CHAPTER NINE

JAMES PAYNTON EMERGED from behind the farmhouse. He was a short man, with a bald pate and a broad, round nose. His puffy cheeks revealed deep dimples whenever he smiled, which he did, frequently.

"Hello there!" he called as Annabelle and the inspector walked towards him. "Inspector Nicholls, I presume."

The two men shook hands, then James directed his smile at Annabelle. "Reverend, it's nice to see you. I wasn't expecting you, too."

"We bumped into each other on the way," Nicholls explained.

"I helped him find your, um, farm," Annabelle added.

"Sorry I'm so late," the inspector said.

"It's alright, I understand your job is unpredictable." Paynton smiled.

Nicholls glanced at Annabelle. "It certainly is."

"Good," Paynton said, clapping his hands together. "Shall we?"

"Lead the way," the inspector replied as they proceeded to walk over to one of the barns.

"So, as I told you over the phone," Paynton began, the inspector walking beside him, Annabelle trotting a half-step behind as she absorbed the rather pleasing surroundings, "I breed three types here: Bernese mountain dogs, border collies, and basset hounds—though the hounds are exclusively for hunters. I have a waiting list for those, so if that's what you're looking for you're out of luck, I'm afraid."

They reached the barn. It was a huge, long rectangular building that seemed to radiate warmth. They walked through the open entrance, the gravel of Paynton's driveway giving way to straw underfoot.

"The dogs have access to an indoor and outdoor area. They tend to wander in and out depending on the weather, their temperament, and inclination. I usually allow the dogs the run of the field, whilst the puppies are kept in a smaller pen. If it's raining, they are kept inside, separated by breed, of course, though I do let them mingle every once in a while; it keeps them stimulated. I've kept them in the pens today so you can take a good look at them. I'd just about given you up, so it's lucky you arrived when you did. I was about to let them all out."

Two large pens were set against the long wall of the barn. In one, two gigantic yet composed dogs lay lazily on the ground. They raised their heads on seeing the visitors, their thick, shaggy fur hanging off their bodies like luxurious blankets. Around them, a half-dozen smaller versions scampered and played. Paynton walked up to a gate and unlatched it.

"These are the Bernese mountain dogs," he said, holding the gate open for the inspector and Annabelle. The puppies gazed at the intruders doubtfully for a moment before one adventurous pup crawled over to Annabelle and flopped down next to her. She immediately tickled his tummy.

"Oh, they're simply gorgeous!" Annabelle squealed.

Seeing their littermate receive such attention, the rest of the puppies ran over. The inspector bent down and playfully rolled his hand around the puppies' thick coats.

"These pups are knocking on three months, now," Paynton said, observing the scene, fists on his hips, "so they're ready to be rehomed. To tell you the truth, these are my favourites. Very intelligent, very *sympathetic* dogs."

The inspector stood and backed away to stand next to Paynton, watching as one of the adult dogs lumbered over to Annabelle.

"Oh! Aren't you a friendly fellow!" she said, still crouching as she was greeted by the dog. A large, thick pink tongue licked her neck. The dog panted and shook a little. Annabelle felt a warm, light shower douse her face.

"Are they strong dogs?" the inspector asked as the big dog pressed its body evermore affectionately against Annabelle's shoulder. She put a hand out to steady herself.

"Strong as an ox, though you wouldn't know it, what with how gentle they are."

"Hmm," the inspector said as he watched Annabelle push the dog away and stand upright, noticing that the dog was level with her hip. "Rather big, aren't they?"

"Oh, absolutely," Paynton replied. "Big in all senses of the word. Big brains. Big hearts. Big coat of fur. Why? Is that a problem?"

"Well, my place isn't small, but it's no farmhouse either," Nicholls said, looking around him.

"I understand," Paynton said, snapping his fingers and

turning quickly. "Come with me. I'll show you the border collies."

The inspector followed Paynton out of the barn without looking back. Later he told Annabelle he had no idea that the adult Bernese had leapt up and placed its paws on her shoulders.

"Now this is more like it!" the inspector said as he leant over a fence and caught sight of the excited, playful collies in the next barn.

"I trust you're familiar with this breed?" Paynton said, unlatching the gate and stepping through into the pen.

"Indeed I am," Nicholls said, following him and immediately crouching to play with the pups. "Come here, you!"

"Well, there are seven puppies, two haven't been reserved yet. This one over here with his ears in the air, and that one by your left foot."

"Ah, this one?" the inspector said, immediately ruffling the ears of the one next to him. "Oh, this one looks a right little scamp—*aren't you?*"

"I'm happy to let you have one, but these were only born eight weeks ago. They'll need to stay here for a while longer. I don't let my pups go until the tenth or preferably twelfth-week mark."

Nicholls stood up. "That sounds reasonable to me."

"Great," Paynton said as they left the pen, and he closed the gate behind him. They ambled out of the barn into the cool air.

"So what should I do? Come back in a few weeks?"

"Well, usually I'd ask for a deposit and then let you know when I feel the puppy is ready to go, but seeing as it's you, Inspector, I don't think there will be any need for that. I'll give you a call when he's ready, and if you're still interested, he's yours."

Nicholls smiled gratefully. "I can't really ask for a better deal than that, can I? Thank you, James."

"No problem," the dog breeder beamed. "Hey, where is Annabelle?"

The two men scanned their surroundings before their gaze settled on the first barn. With impeccable timing, Annabelle staggered out of the open entrance, squinting in the daylight. She was hazily brushing at her clothes as she looked around her. Her disordered hair seemed to have been thrown in every direction, having gathered numerous strands of straw. They stuck to her like she was a scarecrow.

"Are you okay, Reverend?" Paynton called as they walked towards each other.

"Oh yes! Fine! Fine!" Annabelle said breathlessly. She wiped her face. "A rather playful chap, that dog."

"He must have taken a shine to you, Reverend! " Paynton smiled. "He's a very good judge of character."

Annabelle grimaced. "He's terribly heavy, too," she said, pressing her shoulder.

Nicholls couldn't restrain himself any longer. He suddenly let out a deep belly laugh. "Reverend," he said, "perhaps I should be adopting you, rather than a dog!"

CHAPTER TEN

ANNABELLE WAS STILL smoothing herself down and combing out the debris from her hair when the inspector pulled up behind her Mini Cooper. It was parked neatly on the roadside where she had left it. He put on the handbrake with a sharp click and turned to face her in the passenger seat.

"Are you sure you wouldn't like me to wait for the tow truck?"

"Absolutely not, Inspector," replied Annabelle. "You've got a murder investigation to conduct, and you've already wasted an hour visiting a dog breeder!"

"Hmph," snorted the inspector. "I have faith that my constables will follow procedure. I'm most useful when it's time for initiative. Besides, I've got a funny feeling about this case."

"A 'hunch,' as they say in the movies?"

"Something like that."

"What is it?"

The inspector took a deep breath. When he had first met Annabelle, this would have been the moment at which he would have told her that this was police business and that she had no reason to get involved. Looking at her now, however, and knowing her genuine compassion and dedication to every member of her community, he realised that she had become a valuable companion whenever his work brought him to Upton St. Mary. Her love for people and her astute understanding of human nature were appreciated assets. Her lack of conceit and gentle humour was a refreshing change from the kinds of behaviour—those of criminals and officious colleagues—that he normally had to deal with. It occurred to him that these visits to Upton St. Mary and specifically the time he spent in Annabelle's company had become a welcome respite for him. A place in which he felt welcomed, relaxed, and a little more human.

"I think Mildred's death is part of something bigger," he said slowly.

"How so?"

"As I say, it's just speculation on my part, but do you remember what you told me earlier? About today turning into a strange day? About the car with blacked-out windows, the breakdown, the rumours?"

"Of course."

"Well, I had my own strange encounter earlier. Whilst I was in the pub preparing to meet James, I saw two men, well-known criminals. I would recognise them anywhere, and I'm sure they recognised me. They operate mostly in Falmouth, and I have no idea what they're doing in Upton St. Mary."

"Murderers?"

"No," Nicholls said, shaking his head, "but they *are* versatile. Drugs, prostitution, stolen goods; anything they can make a little money from."

"Oh dear," Annabelle murmured at the thought of such criminality in heavenly Upton St. Mary.

"Don't worry about it, Reverend," the inspector said. He changed his tone. "They've probably just met some women here or needed to hide out for a bit. They might even have simply been having a quiet pint."

"Well, if you think so . . ." Annabelle said, unconvinced, before getting out of the car. "Thank you for everything, Inspector."

"My pleasure, Reverend."

Ian Crawford, the owner of Crawford Motors, was a smug, arrogant man. He was muscular, broad-shouldered, and he walked with the swagger of an overly aggressive alpha male. His strong jawline seemed the result of constantly clenched teeth. He stared menacingly, even when he was joking. No one ever laughed at his jokes, but it didn't stop him from making them.

As she thanked the driver and stepped out of the tow truck, Annabelle remembered something she had heard about Crawford's dubious past. It was suspected that he was a purveyor of stolen cars. Despite this, she had visited Crawford Motors multiple times before and although she found the owner's personality somewhat abrasive, she had no complaints about his mechanical skills. Once her Mini Cooper was unhooked from the tow truck and sitting in the lot, Annabelle walked into the large four-bay garage.

"Hello, Miss Dixon," said the unmistakably slow, slithery voice of Ian Crawford. He pushed himself out from beneath a nearby car and grinned, unashamed of his remarkably crooked, yellow teeth.

Annabelle opened her mouth to correct his addressing her as "Miss" before remembering that she did so to no avail every single time she visited his garage. It was entirely likely he did it on purpose.

Crawford stood up and crossed himself. Annabelle smiled calmly at his little joke. It took much, much more to faze her. She said nothing because, in her view, in the battle between vengeful response and polite decorum, the latter always won.

"Hello, Ian," she said, with the same warmth she used to greet children. "I'm here to get my car fixed."

"Of course. Just like everybody else in Upton St. Mary."

"What do you mean?"

Crawford grinned again before pointing at the cars at the other end of the lot. "Greg Fauster's Punto. Danielle Welbeck's Audi. Harry Loftus' Honda. And now your Mini. All of you came in this morning. First time I've seen any of you in a long time. What's going on?"

"Something bad has happened to Mildred."

"Oh?" Crawford said, still smiling broadly.

"She's dead."

His face dropped, and he gulped. "Huh. Interesting."

"The police are investigating."

Crawford squinted. "Investigating? Why?"

Whether it was the guilt of having given his name to the inspector, her irritation at Crawford's obnoxious behaviour, or an attempt to gauge his reaction, Annabelle found herself saying the next few words without much forethought.

"It would appear she was murdered. They think it could be a competitor," she said impulsively.

Crawford revealed his ugly smile slowly this time. "Me? Ha! Now isn't that something! Well, I hope the coppers do come by and ask me a few questions, actually."

Annabelle frowned. "Why would you want that?"

Crawford's laugh was abrupt and throaty. "I'd soon set them straight!"

"What do you mean?"

Crawford stuck a tongue in his cheek with a sense of mischief before nodding at Annabelle's Mini behind her. "What's wrong with your car?" he said as he walked over to it.

"It broke down whilst I was driving. But back to—"

"Did the engine just stop working suddenly?"

"Yes. What do you mean abo—"

"And before that, it wouldn't respond to the accelerator? It kept trailing off? Coming and going?"

"Yes."

Crawford nodded as he opened the flap to the Mini's fuel tank and unscrewed the cap. "And the last place you got petrol was at Mildred's?" he said, though it clearly wasn't a question to which he expected a negative answer.

Annabelle watched with a furrowed brow as Crawford leant his head over the open fuel tank and sniffed. "Yep," he said, nodding to himself. "Hey, Gary! Come over here. We've got another one."

From inside the garage, a husky teenager with an acne-riven face loped towards his boss. Ian Crawford pointed at the Mini.

"What you reckon?" Crawford asked.

The teenager, much the same as his boss had done, leant in over the open fuel tank and sniffed. "Yeah, no doubt about it."

"What's going on?" Annabelle asked.

Crawford dismissed the teenager, replaced the fuel cap, and walked back to Annabelle.

"Sugar water. It's been mixed in with the fuel. Just like

every other car that the old bat fuelled up in the past couple of weeks."

The shock of this heinous idea was enough to stop Annabelle from noticing the insult directed at Mildred.

"Why would she do that?"

Crawford shrugged. "No idea. Maybe she went senile. Working on cars at her age shouldn't be allowed, anyway. Maybe she was trying to squeeze out a little more profit or keep people coming in for repairs. The real question is why anyone would get their fuel from the last garage in England to pull it straight out of a barrel. Stupid, if you ask me."

"I can't believe it," Annabelle said, her head spinning with implications.

Crawford laughed again before turning his head and spitting. "It was probably somebody who found out what she was doing that did the old bird in. Judging by how many people are turning up here with wrecked cars, it could have been any one of her customers or even a whole bunch of them."

Annabelle stared at her car, her mind desperately scrabbling to remember anything notable about the last time she had put fuel in the Mini. She had been to Mildred's so many times, it was difficult to remember any one instance specifically, let alone anything that seemed out of place.

"Can you fix it?" she asked. "My car?"

"Yeah. Just need to flush everything out and put something in there that actually burns."

"Thank you," Annabelle said. "Please call me when it's done." Crawford nodded.

Just before she made it out of the garage forecourt, Annabelle turned back to Crawford, who was pulling a stick of gum from a packet. He shoved it into his mouth greedily. "One more thing," she said. Crawford raised his eyebrows. "Have you noticed any cars with tinted windows around here? Those blacked-out ones you can't see through from the outside?"

Crawford smiled one last crooked grin. "It's better not to ask questions about cars like that, Miss Dixon."

CHAPTER ELEVEN

AFTER TAKING A taxi back to St. Mary's, Annabelle marched up the path to her cottage with a head full of tangled thoughts and confusing questions. Only the sight of Biscuit, perched on a low cobbled wall gazing at the two puppies chasing and tumbling over each other distracted her.

"Biscuit! How are you enjoying your new companions?"

The cat responded by lazily getting up and walking in the opposite direction. At the sound of Annabelle's voice, the pups leapt towards her, their wet tongues hanging, their tails wagging. She laughed as she crouched in front of them and rubbed their sides as they clambered over her to lick her face.

As she enjoyed their unbridled attention, Annabelle's thoughts went to the inspector. If only he could experience their scrappy enthusiasm firsthand! She was sure that if he caught a glimpse of them, there would be no way he'd be able to resist their shining eyes and panting smiles.

"What are you pups yapping about? Oh! It's you, Reverend," Philippa said, emerging from the cottage.

"I see Janet still doesn't have space for these rascals yet," Annabelle said, reluctantly pulling herself away from the puppies.

"No," Philippa said, shooing them back inside the cottage, "and you seem rather pleased about it."

Annabelle smiled as she took off her coat and hung it on the rack, feeling the last sting of the outside chill before the warmth of the cottage seeped into her bones. She walked into the kitchen, her nostrils filling with the scent of Philippa's cooking.

"Oh, that smells wonderful! Whatever are you concocting this time, Philippa?"

"Nothing but a shepherd's pie, Reverend, although I am experimenting with some new flavours. I enjoyed making that curry last week!"

"You should be careful, Philippa. If your cooking gets any more experimental, people around here will start thinking you a witch!"

Philippa laughed and waved away the joke as she knelt in front of the oven. "I'm sure there are many who already do, Reverend," she murmured.

Annabelle sat at the table, kicked off her shoes, and stretched out her toes, allowing herself a deep, exhausted groan now that she was back home. She smiled as she watched the puppies trot over to the corner of the kitchen and curl themselves up against the radiator. Philippa sat at the opposite end of the table, where she had laid out a crossword puzzle and a mug of tea.

"I suppose you've already heard about what happened today," Annabelle said, "seeing as you've not asked me why I'm back so late."

Philippa pursed her lips and frowned. "It's terrible. I never knew Mildred that well, not being a driver myself, but

I hadn't heard a bad word said about her in all my days living in Upton St. Mary."

"I know," Annabelle replied wistfully. "This entire day seems like a surreal nightmare. I'm glad it's finally over."

"It's not over yet," Philippa said, her voice knowing and wily.

Annabelle gazed at her friend. "Are you implying that it can get worse?"

"No," Philippa said, a glint in her eye. "I'm saying it can get better."

Annabelle watched a smile form on Philippa's lips. "You're up to something, aren't you!" she said. "What is it?"

Philippa paused and smiled. "I've invited Inspector Nicholls to join us for supper," she said finally.

"What? Why?" Annabelle knew her friend far too well to credit that there wasn't an ulterior motive behind Philippa's invitation. She dreaded hearing what that motivation might be.

Philippa sat upright and spoke haughtily as if she were a judge casting a verdict. "It's about time you and the good inspector grew more acquainted," she said before adding, "on a more *personal* level."

"Philippa!" Annabelle cried, almost leaping onto the table. "We *are* acquainted!"

"You know very well what I mean, Reverend. You're an upstanding, much-respected member of this community, but you can't do everything alone. It would be good for you to have someone you can depend on intimately, someone trustworthy, loyal, determined, and good. Someone like the inspector."

Annabelle shook her head in disbelief, opening her mouth to give voice to the disquiet she was feeling, but finding that words failed her.

"Philippa," Annabelle said, struggling to calm herself down, "the inspector is in the middle of a very serious murder investigation. He doesn't have time for your matchmaking games!"

"Well, the middle of an investigation is the only time the inspector is in Upton St. Mary long enough to play them!" Philippa said.

A deep frown creased Annabelle's brow. "How did you manage to convince the inspector to visit us for dinner, anyway?"

Philippa shrugged. "Oh, that was easy. I simply told him I had important information regarding the investigation."

"Philippa!" Annabelle squealed, her jaw-dropping almost to the table. "How could you? That's . . . that's . . . awfully unlike you! You can't lie to the inspector like that!"

"It's no lie, Reverend."

"What do you mean?"

"I know—" Just then, the doorbell rang. Annabelle jumped. "That must be him now! Why don't you let him in, Reverend? I'll set the table."

Annabelle pursed her lips in disapproval at her church secretary's attempts to play cupid, but she made her way to the door, pausing briefly to straighten her hair in the hallway mirror.

"Inspector!" Annabelle said warmly as she opened the door.

"Hello, Reverend," he replied somewhat shyly.

"Thank you for coming." She waved him inside.

Taking his coat, Annabelle followed the inspector into the kitchen, which Philippa had managed to transform in the seconds it had taken the vicar to go to the front door. No longer was the cosy kitchen lit up by the bright fluorescent ceiling light. Instead, three candles sat in the middle of the table. They cast a warm, flickering glow onto the wood-grained top. The table had been set with red napkins alongside a bottle of red wine that Annabelle hadn't even known was in her possession. She silently suspected it was the bottle previously destined for Sunday's Holy Communion and purloined by Philippa from the church office. Most alarming of all, there were just two plates on the table. They were placed across from one another. Annabelle shot a wide-eyed look at Philippa, who stood at the table with her hands clasped behind her like a maître d' at a fancy restaurant.

"Take a seat, Inspector," Philippa said, formally enunciating every syllable.

"Thank you," he said, sitting in the chair she had pulled out for him. "Won't you be joining us?"

"Oh . . . ah . . . no . . ." Philippa said, suddenly flustered. "My . . . um . . . I just received a call from . . . ah . . . my niece's brother . . ."

"Your nephew?" Annabelle corrected her pointedly, unwilling to let Philippa's floundering attempts to fib pass unnoticed.

"Yes . . . he . . . um . . . needs me . . ."

"I see," the inspector said, growing uneasy at the evidently awkward situation in which he found himself. "You mentioned that you knew something about the case?"

"Ah yes," Philippa said as she picked up the inspector's plate from in front of him and took it to the counter. "It's about Ted Lovesey. The mechanic at Mildred's."

"You know where he is?" the inspector asked. "We haven't been able to locate him."

"Not exactly," Philippa said, placing the plate of steaming hot shepherd's pie in front of him.

"This looks very tasty," the inspector said.

"Oh, our reverend is quite the cook," Philippa said, winking at Annabelle as she took her seat. She received a look of horror in return.

"You were saying?" urged the inspector.

"Yes . . . well . . . every Friday without fail, Ted spends the entire night at the Dog and Duck," Philippa said, placing Annabelle's plate in front of her before quickly making her way to the coat rack in the hall. She returned to the kitchen with her coat. "Except last night he wasn't there."

"Do you have any idea where he went?"

"I'm afraid not, Inspector," Philippa said as she roughly shrugged her thick coat on. "But I can assure you if Ted isn't in the Dog and Duck on a Friday night, something is very wrong." Philippa was now talking rapidly. One might think that she wanted to get out of the cottage as quickly as she could.

"I've had men looking for him all day. Nobody's seen him since Friday afternoon," the inspector muttered.

"Well, I hope you find him soon," Philippa said, breathlessly jamming her woolly hat on her head as she walked swiftly down the hall to the front door. "Cheerio!"

Before Annabelle could even think about calling Philippa back, the sound of the front door slamming echoed through the cottage. She turned to the inspector, wondering if he was feeling as vulnerable as she was on the other side of the flickering candles. She poured them each a glass of wine.

They glanced at each other awkwardly for a few more moments, flashing embarrassed smiles across the table. With every moment that passed, the atmosphere seemed to grow more uncomfortable.

"Did you make any progress today?" Annabelle finally asked.

"No, not much. As well as Ted, the teenager, Aziz Malik, is still missing, and a check on the car that was parked over the top of the pit we found Mildred in turned up nothing."

They exchanged a few more flushed smiles before turning their attention to the food. "This really does look delicious," the inspector said. "I had no idea you could cook."

"Um, yes," Annabelle stuttered, unable to add anything more complex to the conversation. Immediately, she was mortified by her inability to refute the whopper Philippa had propagated about her cooking.

In her confusion, Annabelle grabbed the wine bottle and offered it to the inspector, even though his glass was full. He shook his head. Annabelle nodded in acknowledgement and feeling foolish, put the wine down as they settled back into silence.

After a few more seconds of what seemed to be turning into a game of patience, the inspector picked up his fork. "Well, let's dig in, shall we?"

CHAPTER TWELVE

"UM," ANNABELLE SAID. The inspector looked up. "Philippa can be rather insistent at times. You know, I would understand perfectly if you didn't have the time to stay. You must have an awful lot of work to do."

"No, it's fine. I haven't eaten since breakfast. The last thing I had was a pint of bitter at the Silver Swan, and I didn't even finish that." The inspector looked appreciatively at his plate. "Besides, I doubt I could get a better meal anywhere."

Annabelle smiled warmly, glad that he wanted to stay and that at least some of the awkwardness had evaporated. They began eating, the clink of fork against plate adding some much-needed sound to the silence.

Suddenly the inspector jumped in his seat, his eyes wide in surprise. "Reverend!"

"Yes?"

"I . . . didn't think . . . that you were that kind of . . ." he mumbled, utterly confused.

"Yes?"

"Um . . . never mind," he said, anxiously turning back to his plate. Annabelle shrugged and carried on eating.

"So will you be staying in Upton St. Mary for a few days to handle the case?" Annabelle asked as she blew on her piping-hot mixture of minced beef and potato.

"Yes," Nicholls replied, doing the same. "I'm staying with Constable Raven's mother. She has a room available, so I'll be here at least until Monday."

"That's good to know. I'll be sure to— Oh!" Annabelle jerked back from the table so violently her knee hit the underside. All the plates rattled.

"What is it?" the inspector asked quickly.

"Oh my!" Annabelle said, turning a deep shade of red.

"Reverend?"

"That's very forward of you, I must say!" she said stroking her cheek.

"What is?"

Annabelle bowed her head and smiled. "Nothing. It's perfectly fine."

The inspector watched her for a moment, frowning a little before shaking his head and resuming his meal.

"By the way," he said after swallowing another hefty mouthful, "where are those puppies you mentioned? Did they find space for them at the shelter?"

"Oh no, they're right here." Annabelle turned to the corner that the puppies had made their regular sleeping spot, only to find it empty. "Hmm. That's strange. I wonder where they are."

She leant back in her chair to check the hallway and spun her head around to scan the kitchen. On a whim, she lifted the tablecloth.

"There you are!" The puppies ran out from beneath the table and placed their paws on her lap. Annabelle and the inspector smiled at each other for a full three seconds before breaking out into hysterical laughter.

"I thought that you were—"

"I thought that you were too, but—"

"But it was the puppies!"

"Those rascals nearly gave me a heart attack!"

They continued to laugh, enjoying the release of tension that had built up between them. The puppies, sensitive to the atmosphere, seemed to laugh along with them, wagging their tails excitedly. The female puppy leapt up onto the inspector's lap, and a moment later, the other pup pounced onto Annabelle's.

"I do believe these puppies are angling for some shepherd's pie," Annabelle giggled.

"Would you mind if—"

"Oh no. There's plenty more."

With childlike glee, the inspector took some of the meat in his palm and grinned when the puppy licked it off his hand in seconds.

"You know, Inspector, I don't think I've ever seen you quite so happy."

"I'm much like a dog myself in many respects," he said, taking another handful of beef and offering it to his eager companion. "Excitement and unbridled enthusiasm are infectious. It rubs off on me when it comes around. It's just that I don't see a lot of it in my line of work."

Annabelle sat back and stroked the puppy on her lap as she enjoyed the sight of the inspector feeding the one on his own.

"You certainly wouldn't be short of fun and excitement with that one," she said.

Nicholls glanced at her. "I don't know . . ."

"Why don't you take care of her for the next few days,

whilst you're in Upton St. Mary? Constable Raven's mother has a dog, so she would have no objections, I'm sure."

Nicholls laughed as the dog licked his empty palm. "I'm supposed to be conducting a murder investigation, Reverend. Not pet-sitting!"

"Psshht, she might even help you! She'd make a terribly good sniffer dog. Why, just the other day she found a pair of gardening gloves I could have sworn I'd thrown away."

"Hmm," the inspector murmured as he allowed the pup to nuzzle his neck, "are you sure Mrs. Raven wouldn't mind?"

"I'm absolutely positive."

Nicholls scrubbed the dog's ears and smiled into its big, soppy eyes. "I suppose it couldn't hurt to have a four-legged companion watching my back."

"Wonderful!" Annabelle said, finally satisfied. "That's settled then."

The next morning, no matter how much she attempted to focus on the Sunday service, Annabelle could not shift the peculiarities surrounding Mildred's murder from her mind. It seemed to her like a complex, macabre jigsaw. She felt she already possessed half the pieces but was missing the other half. Even as she spoke to her congregation on the importance of remembrance, her mind was elsewhere looking for threads and themes that might connect all the strange occurrences from the day before.

It was the same after the service. Annabelle stood at the doors of her church, smiling and making small talk to her parishioners as they poured out through its large arched entrance. They were serenaded by Jeremy, the organist. But as she shook hands and engaged her congregation with as much personality and humour as always, Annabelle's mind continued to swirl with the intricacies of the case.

When the last of her parishioners had left, Annabelle decided to take her Mini Cooper for a spin around the lanes to clear her head, before remembering that her car was still at Ian Crawford's garage. She thought about what Crawford had said about the fuel sold at Mildred's. Adulterated with sugar water? Mildred? Surely not.

Annabelle walked back inside the church and slowly made her way to the office where Philippa was waiting for her. Her church secretary always helped her hang her vestments after Holy Communion.

"You're very quiet today, Vicar. Are you alright? How was your evening with the inspector?" Philippa sounded concerned.

"Hmm? Oh, it was fine. Yes, really. Fine."

Philippa looked at Annabelle carefully. "Just fine? Nothing more?" There was no reply. Philippa sighed as she slipped a coat hanger inside Annabelle's white alb.

Annabelle's words came out in a rush. "Oh, Philippa, I'm perplexed. What is going on? Ted's absence from the Dog and Duck is extraordinary. It almost certainly puts him at the top of the inspector's list of suspects!"

"He is a bit of a rum 'un, that Ted, Vicar. I'll give you that. Are you so sure of his innocence? We're all capable of strange deeds when we don't follow the word of the Lord. And he certainly doesn't do that!"

"Yes, I know. He's frequently drunk, driven more by worldly desires than is good for him, but I just can't believe it. There's no logic to it. No money was stolen, no obvious benefit was gained from Mildred's murder. What could have been behind her killing?" Annabelle had racked her brain, but the motive proved to be as elusive as the culprit.

"Ted's disappeared, Vicar. You have to face it. It seems a clear act of guilt."

"More is going on, Philippa. The fuel pumped at Mildred's has been tampered with." Philippa stared at Annabelle, stunned at this news. "Ian Crawford thinks that Mildred did it for monetary gain, but that wouldn't have been like her."

"Do you think Mildred was in trouble, perhaps? Financially, I mean. Perhaps eking out the fuel helped her make ends meet? Small savings can make a big difference. That's why I turn off *all* the lights in the church."

Philippa looked pointedly at Annabelle. The church lights were a bone of contention between them. Annabelle liked to keep a few on at all times, even when the church wasn't being used. Philippa thought it a sinful waste of money.

Annabelle shook her head. "I doubt it. Mildred's Garage always had plenty of work on. Her prices were cheap enough that no one would have objected if she needed to raise them. The financial benefits of stretching the fuel or even fixing the cars that broke down as a result simply wouldn't have been worth it. Perhaps someone devised the scheme to jeopardise Mildred's reputation?"

Philippa looked at the vicar for a long moment. Annabelle, seeing her scepticism, appealed to her. "What about the men disappearing from home for long periods that you mentioned? Perhaps there's a connection there?"

"Now, now, Vicar. I'm sure there's a simple explanation for that. Why don't I make you a nice cup of tea?"

"Thank you, Philippa, but I must get on. Sundays can be such busy days." Annabelle made to leave the office.

"Oh." She paused and half turned to Philippa, "I don't suppose you've heard if they've found Aziz yet? The inspector told me last night that he was still missing, too."

"No, nothing, Vicar, sorry."

"The inspector went to see his parents, you know. He had a difficult time, poor man. Their English isn't the best." Annabelle looked at the floor as if it were a map on which she'd find buried treasure, perhaps in the form of answers to her questions. "But they are such lovely people! Surely Aziz couldn't be involved?"

"He's certainly a good boy from all accounts. Mrs. Whitbread says he always helps her with her groceries and won't accept anything but thanks in return." Philippa was now carefully laying Annabelle's stole in a drawer. Annabelle leant against her desk. "According to the inspector, his parents said that Aziz spends much of his time out of the house, studying at the library, riding his bike, and socialising with friends."

"Sounds like a typical teenage boy to me," Philippa murmured as she closed the drawer.

"And he often spends weekends sleeping over at his schoolmates' houses after particularly gruelling study sessions. But he hasn't been seen since teatime on Friday. His parents told the inspector that they didn't know what he had been doing or where he was."

"What about his phone? He must have a phone. All the young ones do these days."

"Not answering it. The inspector thinks it is all rather suspicious, but I think there must be a simple explanation. It just doesn't feel right to me. Oh, Philippa, it is so vexing!"

CHAPTER THIRTEEN

ANNABELLE'S THOUGHTS CONTINUED to whirl around her brain like screaming banshees. When she started to feel dizzy and saw spots before her eyes, she realised she needed to calm herself down. She went outside and stood on the church steps. She breathed in the cold, damp air for a few moments, feeling refreshed by its invigorating chill. Shortly, Annabelle turned back to the church and walked to the pulpit, calmer but still deep in thought. Jeremy was at his organ, sifting through sheets of music.

"Hello, Jeremy," Annabelle said, reassured by his stable, reliable presence.

"Oh, hello, Vicar," Jeremy replied. He put his music down and turned to face Annabelle, giving her the full respect he always afforded her. "You led a remarkable service today. Thank you."

"I'm glad you thought so, Jeremy, although honestly, I was terribly distracted all morning."

"What's bothering you, Vicar? If I may be bold enough to ask," he added.

"It would be quicker to tell you what *isn't* bothering me," Annabelle said with a humourless laugh. "Frankly, I had enough to concern me before all this dreadful business with Mildred: the cemetery renovation, my car breaking down, and what we're going to do with those puppies!"

Jeremy shifted in his seat and gave Annabelle a sympathetic look. "What seems like a problem is often a blessing in disguise, Vicar."

"Yes, that's true," Annabelle said wistfully. She stood up a bit straighter. "Thank you, Jeremy, I should know that, shouldn't I?"

"I'm sorry, Reverend Dixon," the organist said, hanging his head. "You're the last person to whom I should be offering guidance. Please excuse me. I was being presumptuous."

Annabelle laughed softly. "Don't be so bashful, Jeremy. Your advice is welcome and much appreciated. And spot on. I'm sure that once these travails are put to rest, we'll all emerge stronger and wiser."

Jeremy's grin was wide and boyish, like that of a boy scout receiving yet another badge. "Thank you, Vicar. You are most sensible." Annabelle chuckled at this rather archaic compliment.

"Oh," Jeremy continued, "I almost forgot. I do have some good news."

"Yes?"

"Your car—a Mini, I believe? It's been repaired. Ian Crawford told me that you can pick it up today if you like."

"Ah! That's wonderful," Annabelle said, clapping her hands. "At least I won't have to ride a bike in this weather. A bad case of the sniffles would *really* not be a blessing at this point!"

"I agree with you there, Vicar."

"So you visited Crenoweth?" Annabelle said.

"No, I saw Mr. Crawford here, in Upton St. Mary, last night."

Annabelle scratched her head and pursed her lips. "Really? Strange . . ."

"What is, Vicar?"

"I don't believe Ian Crawford is the sort of chap for whom there is anything of interest in Upton St. Mary. In fact, I've never seen him here in all my time serving at the church. I'm surprised, Jeremy, that you and he are acquainted. I wouldn't have thought you two have much in common."

"I'm sorry, Vicar," Jeremy said, his long fingers fidgeting in his lap. "I do hope I haven't given you any further cause for concern."

"Don't be silly," Annabelle said. She was about to start ruminating again but quickly stopped herself. "I pretty much reached my full capacity for worry long ago!"

🐾

Annabelle was glad that the cab ride she was taking to Crenoweth would be her last—at least for the foreseeable future. She had never enjoyed the experience of being a passenger very much and would often find herself pressing phantom pedals when sitting in the passenger seat. At her worst, she would silently sit and judge the driver's skills—their heaviness on the brakes, inability to accelerate smoothly, inexpert steering skills, and clunky gear changes. She knew backseat driving wasn't her most positive trait.

In between silently critiquing the cab driver's handling

of his taxi, Annabelle thought about what she would ask Ian Crawford once she reached his garage. The mechanic came across as shifty and devious at the best of times and seemed to revel in his ability to arouse suspicion in others. Whilst Annabelle refused to respond to his provocations, she could not dismiss the deeply bothersome idea that Crawford had visited Upton St. Mary recently. It was most unlike him. Annabelle knew for a fact that, when called out to the village by some unfortunate car owner who needed his services, Ian Crawford sent one of his mechanics rather than come out himself. So why had he visited the village the night following Mildred's murder? Annabelle would ask him a few questions.

Her prepared inquisition was for naught, however. Crawford was not to be found at the garage. Instead, the same husky teenager who had sniffed out her Mini's problem on her previous visit emerged from the office to present her with the keys and a bill for the repair.

When asked about his boss's whereabouts, the teenager merely shrugged, and offered a mumbled reply. "He don't work Sundays."

Dissatisfied and with a sense of anticlimax, Annabelle paid her bill. As she walked to her Mini, however, her excitement at getting behind the wheel again hit her with a rush. She turned the key in the ignition, and closed her eyes with pleasure when the Mini responded with a loud purr. The car was like an old pet seeing its master for the first time after an absence. Annabelle took her time settling into the well-worn seat and savoured the feeling of the steering wheel's leather under her hands. When she was ready, and with some ceremony, she released the handbrake. Seconds later, she was off, a wide smile spread across her face.

As the leafless trees zipped by and the Mini ate up the

curling roads, Annabelle revelled in her freedom. She smoothly changed gears and skilfully steered around blind corners. She revved powerfully away from junctions. Her mind turned again to the events of the past twenty-four hours. This time, boosted by being behind the wheel of her beloved car, her thoughts seemed sharper. They were more focused as if by regaining control over her car, she had regained control over her mind. She began to see a pattern as she mulled points one by one.

Both Ted and Aziz had disappeared at roughly the same time. They remained missing. Ian Crawford, a man ill-suited to the routine and provincial nature of village life, along with a couple of criminals known to the inspector, had turned up in the village with no particular reason to do so. Moreover, the village's men were out of the house more than usual and keeping money from their wives. Admittedly, this was a rumour, but it seemed at least a little more meaningful than the usual tittle-tattle. To these unusual events, Annabelle added her sighting of the car with blacked-out windows and the sheer outlandishness of Ted's absence from the pub on a Friday night. Annabelle looked for commonalities and after mulling it all over, became convinced that something was seriously afoot regarding the *men* of Upton St. Mary.

Annabelle thought about what to do. She didn't have to think for long. The next step was obvious. As with anything concerning the men in the village, there was one place she was sure to find an answer: The Dog and Duck.

Annabelle parked her car on a cobbled street a little way down from the inviting, old-fashioned pub. She got out of her Mini and walked towards the pub but not before stopping to cast one last smile at her sorely missed but now reclaimed vehicle. Inside, the pub was already busy with the loud, elbow-to-elbow business of the Sunday lunch crowd.

Annabelle slid through the drinkers in a haze of greetings, seeing many of them for the second time that day, glasses of red wine in their hands. No doubt, she thought wryly, they were continuing their celebration of the Blood of Christ, the bar presumably substituting for the Communion table this time. When Annabelle reached the bar, the short but unmissable, busty, blonde, beehived bartender that she was hoping to see was there.

"Reverend!"

"Hello Barbara," Annabelle said to the bubbly pub landlady.

"It's always a lovely surprise to see you here," Barbara said in her high, musical voice. "Would you like something to eat?"

Annabelle cast a quick glance at the pub's filled-to-bursting booths. "I doubt I could find a seat even if I did! No, thank you."

"Something to drink? Orange juice?"

"Thank you, but no. I just wanted to drop by and ask you something quickly."

"Oh, of course, Reverend," Barbara said, leaning her elbows on the bar.

"Actually, it's somewhat private."

"Ah! Come on through to the back then," Barbara said, moving over to the end of the bar and lifting the hatch.

Annabelle slid through the gap, and followed Barbara's platinum-blond hair into the back of the pub. There, a small passage with stairs led to Barbara's quarters above. Another door led to the storage room.

"We won't be disturbed here. So what's the matter, Reverend?" Barbara asked, her long eyelashes fluttering with concern.

"Well, it's probably nothing, and I'm sorry to take up your time when you're as busy as this but—"

"Oh, forget it, Vicar." Barbara laughed, nodding at the crowded pub. "These men can wait for their drinks. They don't know how to pace their drinking, most of them! You're doing me a favour!"

Annabelle chuckled. "Do you happen to know Ian Crawford?"

"The mechanic down in Crenoweth? Of course. My sister lives there."

"Was he in here last night, by any chance?"

"Ian? No. In fact, the only time I can remember seeing him here was when we had that darts competition a few years ago. Oh, he kicked up a heck of a fuss about the entry fee when he lost! I've half a mind not to let him in ever again!"

"Hmm," Annabelle said. "Have you noticed any new people visiting the pub? Men who rarely come here? I know I'm not being very clear about this but—"

"Let me stop you there, Reverend. I know what this is about."

"You *do?*"

"Yes," Barbara said, putting one long, brightly-coloured nail to her lips and frowning. "It's about those rumours, isn't it? The men running off and not going home until the early hours, in daylight sometimes!"

"Yes! You know something about it?"

Barbara nodded ominously. "I can't tell you much,

Reverend. But I can tell you one thing for sure. They're not spending all that time in my pub. Don't be fooled by that lunch crowd out there. Come evening, this place will be virtually empty, and it has been like that every night this week."

CHAPTER FOURTEEN

TRY AS HE might to remain as officious as possible and act with as much professional distance as his role demanded, the inspector couldn't stop smiling like a young boy in a sweet shop whenever he looked at his furry companion. After his meal with Annabelle, Inspector Nicholls had spent much of the night playing with the puppy in his rented room at Mrs. Raven's and already felt they had developed a rapport. By two in the morning, he had taught the dog to sit on her hind legs when he raised his palm. Pleasantly surprised at both the pup's intelligence and his own mentoring capabilities, Nicholls realised he was already impossibly infatuated with the dog.

"Damn that vicar woman!" he muttered, smiling as he gave the mutt another playful scrub behind the ears. "She *knew* I'd never be able to give you back!"

Having quickly and almost completely overcome his initial resistance to adopting a rescue dog, the inspector settled into bed and allowed the puppy to make her own on top of the quilt by his feet.

Now, on this clear, cool Sunday morning, the inspector was up brighter and earlier than the pup. She looked at him curiously through groggy, lidded eyes as he readied himself for the day. Nicholls had been careful to make sure his work wasn't impacted by his doggie diversions, but he still felt that he had wasted far too much time. It had been less than twenty-four hours since the discovery of Mildred's body, but he would have expected to make at least some progress in that time. So far, he had only added more questions to the many that surrounded Mildred's death, and it was time to find some answers.

After retrieving some giblets and bones for the pup from Mrs. Raven's fridge and wrapping them in sheets of newspaper, the inspector made his way to the village police station in the light of dawn. He had attached the lead Annabelle had given him and the puppy followed eagerly at his heels, a noticeable bounce in her step. She smelled something fresh and raw coming from the bag he was carrying.

Nicholls wondered as he walked along what Annabelle was doing that very moment. He surmised that she was probably preparing for her Sunday morning service. He had no difficulty imagining her standing in the pulpit, charming a crowd of villagers with her smile, and discussing matters of the soul in her engaging and compassionate manner.

"I really should check the church out for myself, one of these days," he murmured as he pushed open the doors of the police station and held them wide for the pup to pass through. "Not today, though. Today I've got other matters to attend to."

Nicholls greeted the night-shift officer, ignoring her curious look when she noticed he had company. He made his way to the small side room he appropriated when he worked there. After carefully setting the dog's food in the corner alongside a bowl of water, he watched for a few moments as the puppy tucked eagerly into her meal. He then went to sit behind his desk to take his own breakfast: a cup of poisonously strong tea and all the reports his officers had made regarding the case so far.

"It's looking pretty empty," he muttered, presumably talking to the dog, the only other living, breathing creature in the room. "I'm not seeing any connections." He still had Harper's initial report on the murder weapon and time of death to guide him, but even her astute observations could not help him if he had nothing to link them.

"No apparent motive. No clues unknowingly left at the scene. Seems like premeditated murder to me. Cold-blooded, don't you think?" he said, raising his eyes to the puppy. She looked over from her doggie feast and held his gaze with the same intelligence and curiosity with which she always seemed to regard him. Her ears lifted, and she cocked her head.

Nicholls laughed and turned back to his papers. The key had to lie with Ted or Aziz. He still had some hope that Aziz would turn up, but Ted's disappearance troubled him, especially after hearing Philippa's assertion that he never usually missed his Friday night drinking sessions.

Rather than focusing on all the possible avenues concerning Ted's disappearance, however, the inspector found his mind wandering to his meal with Annabelle. He sat back in his chair, tea mug in hand, a slight smile on his face as he reminisced the previous evening, utterly distracted from the important matter that lay on his desk.

"She's really quite a remarkable woman when you think

about it," Nicholls said as the puppy having finished her meal, padded over to him and curled up beside his chair. "To be a vicar in a village such as this and to still have such good street smarts. She's really rather astute, you know, a fine set of instincts—if a little overzealous at times." He paused before resuming his one-sided chat with the dog. "It's rather interesting to talk to her, you know. I spend so much time dealing with the very worst aspects of people that I rarely think of their better qualities. The vicar is pretty clever in bringing out the good side in those around her, wouldn't you agree?" Nicholls looked down at the puppy beside him, who lazily raised an eyebrow. "Yes, they don't make them like the reverend very often, that's for sure," he said with a sigh. "To be honest, the first time I met her, I thought that she was rather bumbli—"

"Yes, Inspector?" came a pleasant voice from the doorway. Nicholls jumped. "Did you call me?" PC McAllister stood at the threshold to the inspector's office.

"Oh yes," the inspector began, quickly sitting upright and guiltily sifting through his papers. "Yes, I did. Come in and sit down a moment, would you, McAllister?"

Police Constable Jenny McAllister was a relatively new recruit to the Upton St. Mary police force. She was a young officer, sympathetic and bubbly, with a deep respect for her superiors. Despite still learning the ropes, she had displayed an enormous talent for dealing with people. Confronted with her big, blue eyes and her genuine smile, members of the public found themselves softening, opening up, and often forgetful of whatever bother had brought them into contact with a police officer in the first place.

Jenny McAllister also had another skill that set her apart from her peers. She had an uncanny flair for organisation. No one was faster, more thorough, or more meticulous in completing the paperwork that accompanied police duties than Jenny. Soon, she had flipped the tables on her more senior colleagues who deferred to her whenever unsure of best practices, correct procedure, and greatest efficiencies.

As a new, and therefore lowly police officer, Jenny had been given plenty of night shifts, a hectic and unpredictable duty in many places, but a predictably quiet one in Upton St. Mary. Not the most popular shift, she had taken them on with good grace and a cheerful smile. She had used this quiet time to make the management of the small police station her own. If something were to happen, no one could coordinate a better response. Jenny had an almost telepathic ability to know where the other officers in Upton St. Mary were, and who would be most suited to respond at any particular moment. This, along with her impeccable trustworthiness, meant that she was frequently allowed to watch the police station by herself.

Jenny smiled as she took the seat opposite the inspector's desk and sat down. "How can I help you, Inspector?" she said.

"You grew up in Upton St. Mary, didn't you?" Nicholls said, clutching some papers and pushing all thoughts of Annabelle and her wonderfulness aside.

"I did indeed."

"Do you know Ted Lovesey at all?"

McAllister shrugged her small shoulders. "I suppose. He spends most of his time at the pub."

"I know," the inspector grumbled. "Do you know if he has a car?"

"Oh, no," McAllister said, with certainty. "He drinks far

too much for that. I suppose that's sort of funny—a mechanic who barely drives."

"Hmm," the inspector said, nodding. "How does he get to work then?"

McAllister put a finger to her lips and frowned as she searched the vast database that was her mind.

"Well, I've seen Greg Bradley pick him up a few times, so perhaps Greg gives him a lift to work? Greg's a firefighter. The fire station isn't too far from Mildred's. They're an odd couple, but they live almost next to each other. Greg doesn't drink at all. He doesn't even eat meat." McAllister stopped suddenly, blushing slightly. "Just a guess, sir. About the lifts, I mean. He might even walk. It's not far. Nothing's far in Upton St. Mary."

Nicholls raised an impressed eyebrow at the young woman across the desk. He dropped his papers on the table and sat back. "You've achieved more in a couple of minutes than I have all morning. Keep that sort of thing up, and you'll be sitting where I am sooner than you think."

McAllister's blush transformed into a beam of delight at the compliment. "Thank you, Inspector!"

"Have we sent anyone to question this . . . Greg Bradley?"

"No, we haven't," she said, turning serious again. "I can do that, but we've only got two other officers on duty right now. Constable Raven is guarding the crime scene at Mildred's and Constable Harris is investigating reports of an illegally parked mobile library on Crowley Street."

"Send Harris to question him when he's done," Inspector Nicholls said, rising from his chair. "I'll go and tell Raven to come back here. We're not going to get much more out of that garage."

Nicholls walked over to the coat rack and put on his

trench coat. To the puppy's great excitement, he picked up the dog lead and attached it to her collar. McAllister stood up with him and moved to the door, but not before the inspector could utter one more compliment in her direction.

"I meant what I said, McAllister. You've got a spark I've not seen in a while—not in a police officer, at least."

CHAPTER FIFTEEN

STILL SATISFIED FROM her earlier meal, the small, brown puppy remained alert but calm as she sat on the front passenger seat of the inspector's car. She appeared to be quietly taking in everything going on around her. The inspector mulled over what a suitable name for her might be as he drove through the morning light of an Upton St. Mary Sunday. Constable Raven spotted the inspector's car from his guard post in the garage office and wandered out to greet him.

"Morning, Raven," the inspector said.

"Morning, Inspector," the constable replied before glancing at the inspector's furry companion. "Is that your dog, sir?"

"It might be," Nicholls replied.

Knowing that even this brief reply was more than the inspector usually gave in response to questions he regarded as personal, Constable Raven set aside his curiosity for the time being.

Nicholls stepped under the crime scene tape and walked slowly to the workshop, looking casually around as if he might stumble across something he had previously missed. Raven followed half a step behind.

"So did you notice anything overnight, Raven?"

"No, sir. Didn't hear or see a thing. Not even a mouse squeak."

"Hmm. Well, you should lock up and get yourself back to the station then," Nicholls said, pulling the puppy gently to him. "I think we've got everything we're going to get from this place. Leave the tape up, and check in on it from time to time."

"Yes, sir," Raven said. He was distracted. His eyes were fixed on the puppy. "Er . . . Inspector?"

"Yes?"

"Forgive me if I'm speaking out of turn, but it looks like your friend here is interested in something." The constable nodded at the dog.

Nicholls looked down at the pup he had absent-mindedly been tugging closer to him and saw that she had her nose to the ground. She was sniffing enthusiastically.

"Oh yes," the inspector remarked. "So she is." He suddenly felt as proud as the father of a newborn. He bent down to put his hand under the puppy's chin. He looked into her eyes. "What is it, girl?"

Nicholls loosened his grip on the lead as the puppy jerked her head away, keen to get on with uncovering the source of her interest. The two men followed the puppy outside as she led them in a zig-zag pattern around the garage. After leading them to five large barrels stacked up against the rear of the building, the puppy began sniffing the containers before recoiling with a rapid shake of her head.

"What are these?" the inspector asked his constable.

"They're fuel barrels," Raven replied, watching the

puppy. He grimaced. "The ones we found that were tampered with. I checked them myself based on a tip-off from the vicar. They come from a fuel depot all the way in Newquay. I've asked one of the officers there to check the depot out."

After sniffing around the barrels a little longer, the puppy pulled the men away. She quickly trotted to a corner where a high, sturdy fence separated the garage from its neighbour. There, the ground was piled high with old car parts and boxes. Within a few minutes and after many changes of direction and dead ends, the puppy honed in on a small, red fuel can that sat at the edge of the pile.

"Do you think is it, Inspector? The source of the problem?"

"Let's find out," Nicholls replied. He took out his handkerchief and threaded it through the fuel can's handle. He sniffed slowly at the open spout. "Smells like some kind of soft drink."

He offered it for Raven's olfactory inspection. The constable sniffed and immediately pulled away in disgust.

"Ugh! That's not like any soft drink I've ever had! It's so sweet, it's nauseating!"

Nicholls nodded. "Sugar water," he said. "You can call off your friends in Newquay—whoever tampered with the fuel did his dirty work right here."

"So it must have been one of the mechanics!" Raven said triumphantly.

"Not necessarily," Nicholls replied, immediately curtailing his officer's rather premature celebration. He looked at the fence that circled the garage. "Somebody could have climbed over that with a little effort."

"I suppose you're right," Raven said with a sigh.

Nicholls handed him the fuel can. The constable took it

from him carefully, the handkerchief still passed through its handle.

"Get this checked for prints, Raven. Maybe that will tell us which one of us is right."

"Of course, Inspector," Raven said, interrupted by the crackle of his radio. Nicholls watched as the constable answered the call.

"Raven here."

"Constable Raven, is the inspector with you?" It was McAllister.

"I'm here," growled the inspector, leaning in to be heard.

"You might want to come to the station as soon as you can, Inspector," McAllister said, her voice hazy over the radio network. "We've found Ted Lovesey."

CHAPTER SIXTEEN

MINUTES LATER, BOTH Inspector Nicholls' and Constable Raven's cars screeched to a halt outside the Upton St. Mary police station with an urgency that was almost unheard of, especially on a Sunday. The inspector leapt out in such a hurry that he completely forgot about his furry companion lying with her chin on her paws in the passenger seat. She had to employ quick reflexes. The puppy jumped out just before the inspector slammed the door and trapped her inside. Both the she and Constable Raven followed the inspector as he burst through the doors of the small station, a full six feet of determination and energy.

"He's in the interview room," Constable McAllister said on seeing the inspector. She had stood up quickly from behind her desk when she saw him. There was no doubting the inspector's agitation.

"Where was he when you found him?" Nicholls asked, stopping in front of her.

"At Greg Bradley's house, sir."

"Was Greg there?"

"No. Greg's currently working a shift. Constable Harris spoke to him, however. Greg was in the pub on Friday night, but Ted was't there. Greg was as surprised as anyone at that. Apparently, Ted shows up to ask for a lift home at closing time like clockwork."

Nicholls raised an eyebrow. "So what happened? Why wasn't Ted at his own home?"

Constable McAllister shrugged. "Greg seems just as confused as we are. He said Ted turned up on his doorstep yesterday afternoon out of the blue and asked if he could stay a while. He'd looked pretty shaken up, Greg said, so he didn't ask any questions. They just sat around watching TV together. Last night, Greg had to work a long shift and left Ted at home. Since then, it doesn't look like Ted has left Greg's house."

Nicholls frowned. "Well, maybe Mr. Bradley doesn't like to ask questions, but I certainly do," he said as he made his way to the interview room. The puppy followed. The inspector stopped. "McAllister, make sure the dog's entertained, will you? This could take a while."

"Of course, sir."

Inspector Nicholls took a deep breath and went into the interview room. Everything the inspector had heard about the drifting, drunken mechanic had informed his mental picture. Lacking in self-control, hopeless with money, and seemingly no stability in his life apart from his job, Ted Lovesey, Nicholls had concluded, was more of a criminal type than a typical Upton St. Mary local. Just the sort of person the inspector was deeply familiar with.

And yet, seeing him now, sitting behind a simple table, his big round eyes more like those of a frightened kitten than a ferocious killer, the inspector found his expectations challenged. Ted's round, puffy face was childlike. His hair sat lank and thin on his head, mirroring his defeated, submissive body language. The inspector closed the door slowly behind him and walked over to the table.

"Are you Ted Lovesey?"

The man nodded slowly, his hands clasped between his thighs, his shoulders hunched over as if bracing himself for an attack. Nicholls sat down opposite him. Ted's eyes flickered back and forth from the floor to the inspector, unable to meet his eyes for longer than a second.

"I didn't know," he said suddenly, in a soft, quiet voice.

"What didn't you know?" the inspector asked sharply.

"About Mildred. Jenny just told me now—"

"Constable McAllister to you, man."

"Sorry. Constable McAllister. It's just that I've known Jenny—Constable McAllister—since I arrived here, so I've always called her Je—"

"What didn't you know about Mildred?" the inspector interrupted. He wanted to keep the anxious man on track.

"That she died!" Ted said, his lips quivering. His eyes were glassy. His words hung in the air. "I don't believe it! Who could have done that?"

Nicholls shifted in his seat. This was not what he had been expecting. "That's what I'm working to find out," he said. "Let's start from the beginning: Where were you on Friday night?"

Ted gasped and looked again at the floor, his clasped hands increasingly fidgety. Nicholls waited a whole minute for an answer until he realised one wouldn't be forthcoming.

"Well?" the inspector said.

Ted shook his head, a strained expression on his face. "I can't say," he mumbled into his lap.

Nicholls leant forwards. "And why is that?"

"I just can't. I'm sorry."

The inspector frowned again. "Okay. Tell me why didn't you go home yesterday? Why did you go to Greg Bradley's house?"

Now Ted was wild-eyed. "I can't! Please. I'm sorry . . . I can't tell you."

"What's going on, Ted? Are you afraid of something? Someone?" Ted lifted his eyes from the floor, the sheer terror emanating from them plain to see. "Okay," Nicholls said, shifting his tone. "Let's try something else. What do you know about the fuel tampering?"

Ted stopped fidgeting for the first time since the inspector had entered the room. "Fuel tampering?"

Nicholls sighed. "Is that something else you can't talk about?"

"Honestly, I don't know anything about it."

"Sugar water mixed into the fuel from *your* garage."

"But that's ridiculous!" Ted said. "I mean, for a start, sugar water in the fuel tank doesn't stall a car. It's an urban myth."

"What?"

Ted's anxiety faded as he put his hands on the table and leant forwards to explain. "Well, the whole sugar thing is just unnecessary. Just simple, plain water is enough to ruin the petrol in a car."

Nicholls leant back and scrutinised his suspect. He had a tiny smirk on his face. "So you're saying you're too smart to be involved in this fuel tampering scheme and that if you had been responsible, you'd have just used water. Is that supposed to convince me you didn't do it?"

"No. I'm just trying to understand what you're talking about. I'm sorry if I offended you," Ted said, resuming his hunched over position.

Nicholls tapped his finger impatiently on the table as he looked at the man opposite him. He had pinned much of his investigation on this moment. Questioning Ted—and Aziz—had been his top priorities. But whilst it was clear Ted was hiding something, it was even clearer that Ted was not ready to talk about it. Frightened, anxious, and seemingly unaware of what exactly had happened to Mildred, Ted had given him no answers. Nothing, in fact, but more questions. The inspector found himself frustrated. He surprised Ted by standing up and briskly walking out of the interview room.

Constables McAllister, Harris, and Raven were seated at their desks, chattering away and laughing as they played with the puppy between them. When they heard the inspector open the interview room door, they immediately stopped what they were doing. Each spun in their chairs, their faces open and curious, like baby birds anticipating the return of a parent bearing food. Even the dog turned her head to pant in the inspector's direction.

"What did he say, Inspector?"

"Do you think it was him, sir?"

"Shall we get a cell ready?"

Nicholls looked at each of them, then thrust his hands in his pockets and sighed. His shoulders dropped. "He didn't say anything. We just went around in circles a few times. He's scared, badly shaken-up. I'm sure he knows something."

"But you don't think he did it?" Raven asked.

Nicholls looked back at the interview room, biting his lip. "I'm not sure. But if I didn't know any better, I'd say he was a victim rather than a villain."

CHAPTER SEVENTEEN

ANNABELLE PULLED HER car into a tiny parking spot in front of the inspector's vehicle with such a speedy swoop that several passersby brought their hands to their mouths. When she parked efficiently, missing the kerb and the cars on either side with inches to spare, their gasps were replaced with smiles of relief and a new respect for the reverend's driving skills. It wasn't every day you saw your local vicar handle a car like that.

Annabelle's bustling, black-clad figure emerged from the Mini. She quickly made her way into the station. "Is it true?" Annabelle said, the moment she caught sight of Constable Raven behind the reception desk. "Have you found Ted?"

"Yes," said Raven. "But how did you—"

"Oh, everyone in the pub is talking about it," Annabelle said. She was slightly out of breath. "Timmy Trelawny saw him get into a police car outside Greg Bradley's house."

"What were you doing in the pub, Reverend?" McAllister piped up from her desk beyond reception.

"Ah," said Annabelle, "just having a post-church chat with my flock. They were keen to continue Holy Communion. You know, wine." She held up an imaginary glass. "And bread." She shook an imaginary packet of crisps and chortled, snorting slightly.

"What's all this?" Inspector Nicholls said, emerging from his office.

"Inspector!" called Annabelle, marching past the reception desk to meet him. "I heard you found Ted Lovesey finally."

"Yes," the inspector replied.

"I was wondering if I could speak to him. You see, I've been thinking about the case rather a lot, and I think that—"

"Reverend," the inspector said. "He's being held for interrogation!"

"I do hope not, Inspector!" Annabelle cried. "He isn't a terrorist! And I think I know *just* what to ask him if we want to get to the bottom of—"

"Reverend," the inspector repeated. "This is a police matter. You can't just come barging in and demand to interview our suspects! There's procedure to follow. We're trying to solve a murder here. Look, I respect your interest and investment in this, and you've provided us with some valuable information, but right now the best thing for you to do is to leave us to conduct this investigation in a professional, methodical manner."

"But Inspector!" Annabelle cried, gazing at him incredulously. "I'm trying to help!"

"I'm sorry, Reverend, but you shouldn't be here, and you certainly shouldn't be asking to speak to someone helping us with our inquiries."

"Actually, Inspector," said Raven, looking up from the

puppy. She was perched in his lap. "Perhaps the reverend can help us." Nicholls glared at the constable.

"Yes," added McAllister. "If Ted is holding something back, he'd be far more likely to talk to the reverend than any of us."

"You said it yourself, Inspector, he's scared," Constable Harris continued. "But he knows something. Maybe revealing it to us is too dangerous for him."

Nicholls gritted his teeth and scowled. Annabelle smiled apologetically.

"Well, I guess I'm outvoted. I'll give you five minutes, Reverend, but I'm going in with you," he said.

"Of course!" Annabelle replied.

Nicholls turned on his heel and walked briskly over to the interview room, opening the door for the vicar with a combative expression on his face. Annabelle stepped into the room.

"Oh, hello Reverend," Ted said, his tone a mixture of surprise and relief.

"Hello, Ted. How are you?" Annabelle took a seat opposite him. The inspector closed the door, crossed his arms, and glowered at them from the corner of the room. He didn't care to admit it, but he saw the change in Ted's body language immediately.

"I don't know," Ted said, with a sigh. "I can't tell if I'm coming or going."

"Yes, I understand," Annabelle said with a sympathetic smile. "It's been a rather busy weekend."

"I can't believe what's happened to Mildred," Ted said, shaking his head. "It's just . . . I . . . I don't understand."

"None of us do, Ted. That's why we have to help the police so that the person who did this gets their comeuppance. I mean, who knows if they'll try to do it again!"

Ted's eyes widened. "You think they might kill someone else?"

"If they can murder someone as beloved as Mildred, then no one is safe."

"Oh my God!" Ted cried. Annabelle glanced at the inspector who remained stony-faced.

"Ted, you're an intelligent man," Annabelle began. "You know how bad this looks. You don't go to the pub on a Friday evening for the first time in years, Mildred is murdered sometime the following morning, and then you turn up at Greg Bradley's house without going home. Now I don't believe you had anything to do with Mildred's murder, but I'm afraid I might be the only one."

"I didn't do anything wrong!" Ted cried, reaching his hands out over the table as if clutching at hope. "I can't tell you where I went, though. I just can't! Please trust me!"

"You don't have to tell anyone anything, Ted. But if you *don't* tell the inspector where you were, then he really has no option other than to assume you had something to do with the murder. There's very little evidence to the contrary." Ted buried his face in his hands and sobbed uncontrollably.

"How about this," Annabelle continued in a gentle voice. "I tell you what I think might be going on, and you just listen. You don't have to say a word."

Ted lifted his face to look at Annabelle, then at Nicholls, then back again to Annabelle. He shrugged mildly and wiped his tears.

"Okay," he said, slowly. Annabelle smiled, then cleared her throat.

"I believe there is illegal activity occurring in Upton St. Mary. Activity entertaining enough to entice many of the men who live here, yet illicit enough for them to keep it a secret."

Ted raised his chin and narrowed his eyes. His mouth opened slightly. Whether it was in amazement or from anxiety, Annabelle couldn't tell. Either way, she had struck a chord though. She turned briefly and exchanged a look with the inspector. He had stopped glaring.

"Now, I also believe," Annabelle said, "that this activity involves criminal elements from outside the village. Criminals dangerous and organised enough to make a man keep the activity a secret even when faced with a murder charge." Ted's eyes widened even further, the whites revealing the depth of his emotions.

"The only thing that I'm struggling with, Ted, is just what this illegal activity *is*."

Ted was breathing heavily now, but he managed a nervous chuckle. "There are only so many vices, Vicar."

Annabelle grinned. "Indeed, and they haven't changed much since the Bible was written," she said. "One learns just how diverse a man's sins can be from the good book."

Ted opened his mouth as if to speak before shutting it and shaking his head again. He covered his eyes with his hand and sighed.

"Let's see," Annabelle persisted, "it wouldn't be drink. You're quite adequately catered to in that department. It's not women, either. Many of these men have wives, and it's unlikely that even the most dubious of men in Upton St. Mary would be that adventurous. Drugs, perhaps? I can't believe that, myself. That doesn't leave many options."

"Say it, Vicar," Ted challenged, as if unable to endure this torture any longer.

Annabelle looked back at the inspector one more time. He nodded his agreement, and she turned to the forlorn figure on the opposite side of the table. Ted looked beaten-up and exhausted.

"It's gambling, isn't it Ted? The only thing accessible and entertaining enough to tempt the men of Upton St. Mary. The only thing you would find more exciting than a typical Friday night getting drunk at the Dog and Duck or watching England lose again on the big screen."

Ted shook and sighed, and fidgeted, and winced for a long time before finally sitting upright. He looked directly into the reverend's eyes and nodded gently.

Annabelle stood up. "Don't worry, Ted. You didn't tell us a thing." She turned to the inspector. "Did he?" Nicholls bit his lip, glanced between the two of them, and shook his head just as gently as Ted had.

"But what about Mildred's murder, Reverend? Do you think it has anything to with—"

"I don't know, Ted. I don't know." Annabelle looked Ted directly in the eyes. "But I promise you, I'm going to find out."

The inspector closed the interview room door and carefully took Annabelle by the arm. He ushered her into his office to the puzzlement of both his constables and the puppy. He shut the door firmly behind him.

"Reverend! What was *that?*"

"Whatever do you mean, Inspector?"

Nicholls rubbed his brow hard and paced around the room. "I'm trying to solve a murder case!" he said. "And hopefully, in the process, figure out who's tampering with people's fuel. Now I have a *gambling ring* to investigate? Where did you get that idea? From all those strange incidents you were telling me about? Mysterious cars, disappearing men?"

"From a lot of thought and attention to the facts," Annabelle said, defiantly putting her hands on her hips. "And Ted has just confirmed it!"

"Ah yes," Nicholls said, his exasperation turning to sarcasm. "The man who is the prime suspect in a murder investigation just confirmed that he was taking part in a far less serious crime at the time of the murder. What a surprise! If you'd suggested that he'd built a rocket ship and visited Mars during the time Mildred was beaten to death, he'd probably have confirmed that too!"

Annabelle scowled. "Inspector, I am gravely disappointed in your reaction!"

"How is any of this supposed to help me, Reverend? I'm a *detective*. It's my job to answer questions, make connections, and solve cases; not create more of them with wild speculation and gigantic leaps of logic!"

"I'm a woman of the cloth, Inspector," Annabelle said, lowering her voice as she put her hand on the doorknob, readying herself to leave. "And it's my job to understand that in a community such as Upton St. Mary, everything is connected—even when it may appear otherwise. I sincerely hope you understand this simple fact sooner rather than later. Goodbye, Inspector."

CHAPTER EIGHTEEN

"REVEREND, WAIT!" THE inspector ran out of the station just as Annabelle opened the door to her Mini.

He leapt down the steps with an energy that matched the puppy that followed him. He brought himself to a stop in front of the vicar. The inspector hung his head.

"Reverend," he began, "I apologise. I should not have said those things. It was disrespectful of me."

Annabelle raised her chin as she considered him. "I was only trying to help, Inspector."

"I know. But even you must admit, Reverend, that's a pretty giant leap you took there. A *gambling ring?* You'd never mentioned anything of the kind to me before."

"That's because I had not considered anything of the kind before," Annabelle said coolly. "It was only this morning that I realised how it all fit together."

"But why would you surmise such a thing from hearsay about men disappearing for hours and the sighting of a car with tinted windows? They seem rather flimsy bases for such an idea."

Annabelle placed her hands on her hips and pursed her lips at the inspector's refusal to believe in her theory, however polite he now was about it. "I did not surmise it because of those things, Inspector. I came to that conclusion because I happen to know Ted, and the people of this village very well. It may not seem as rational to you as counting facts and sticking them together logically but an understanding of *human nature* is often a far better path to the truth."

The vicar sighed. She shut the car door softly and bent over to briefly scratch behind the puppy's ears before straightening. "If you must know, Inspector," she said, her tone a little softer now, "I had been thinking of such things long before this terrible business with Mildred. In recent months the church has been struggling to raise funds, a rather remarkable fact considering the generosity of the village during even the toughest of times in the past. Of course, these things can happen. However, when I questioned Barbara, she's the landlady at the Dog and Duck, she seemed even more convinced than I that something was afoot. Ted wasn't the only person who seemed too preoccupied to visit her pub. In fact, he was one of the last regulars she had until even he didn't turn up last Friday night." Nicholls frowned and looked away.

"You don't believe me," Annabelle said, noticing the scepticism the inspector was attempting to hide.

"Look at it from my perspective, Reverend," he said. "A vicar trying to understand why she can't raise funds, a pub landlady trying to explain why her pub suddenly seems so unpopular, and a prime suspect seeking an alibi and an excuse for his strange behaviour. Of course, a story to explain away those problems all at once would be appealing—but a *gambling ring*? In Upton St. Mary? It's just implausible! There must be a million other ways to explain it."

"Such as?"

Nicholls barely flinched. "Honestly?" he said, placing a hand gently on the car's roof. "One thing you learn pretty quickly as a detective is that the most boring, unexciting, and ultimately disappointing theory is frequently the most accurate."

"And what is that?"

"I think Ted's our man and that he's a good liar. I think people aren't drinking at the Dog and Duck because of the cold weather or because one of the other pubs in the village has become more popular. And as for your church . . ." Nicholls paused, glancing down at his feet before braving to look Annabelle in the eye again. "I'm afraid it's just a sign of the times, Reverend. People aren't interested. Or not interested *enough* to part with money for your project. Face it."

They gazed at each other for a few moments, the differences in their arguments seeming to play out in the heady tension.

"Look," the inspector said, trying to bridge the gap between them. "Let's just assume that you're right. None of this is bringing us any closer to the *real* mystery: Who killed Mildred, and why?"

Annabelle raised an amused eyebrow. "'Us,' Inspector?"

Nicholls laughed. "I'm sorry, but can you blame me for thinking of you as a fellow investigator?"

"Not at all." Annabelle smiled. "I'm flattered."

"You're certainly correct about one thing, Reverend," the inspector said with all seriousness. "You know the villagers far better than I do, and you're much more effective at getting information out of them. That's why I'd like to ask you to come along with me now."

"Oh? Where to?"

"Aziz's parents," Nicholls said, determined now. "I want to see if he's come home yet, and if not, where the hell he's got to."

The Maliks were Pakistani immigrants who owned a shop a relatively short walk from the police station. Aziz Malik was their son. As Annabelle and the inspector ambled along the cobbled streets of Upton St. Mary, a happy puppy between them on a lead, Annabelle could not shake the feeling that this felt more like a loving couple's Sunday afternoon stroll than two people seeking someone in connection with a murder investigation. The inspector seemed aware of this too, his expression a little bashful as he walked by her side.

"How are you finding the puppy, Inspector?" Annabelle asked as she watched the dog bounce along for a few steps ahead of them, stop for a few seconds to wait, then bounce on happily again.

"Oh, she's pleasant enough company," he said. "She certainly eats a lot. And she does like to go off and sniff in any direction when she catches a scent." He tugged on the lead, urging the puppy forwards as she allowed herself to be beguiled by the wheel of a parked van.

"Well, she's just a pup, Inspector. I'm sure she'll mature quickly alongside you."

"Now, now, Reverend, I'm fond of her, I won't deny that, but I've yet to make up my mind whether I'll adopt her."

"Very well," smiled Annabelle, a knowing glint in her eye.

The Maliks' shop stood on the corner of one of Upton St. Mary's main junctions, among an array of other shops that saw a steady stream of shoppers from dawn until dusk on most days. Unlike the other shops, however, Malik's was open seven days a week. It was the first stop for a vast majority of villagers seeking their morning paper, a bottle of milk, or even a specialist tobacco that Mr. Malik would order on request in his typically accommodating manner.

Next to the shop was a small driveway for deliveries and a garage for the Maliks' minivan. Annabelle noticed that there was a new, smaller car in the driveway as they walked past, one she had not seen before.

The inspector attached the puppy's lead to a lamp post outside the shop and told her to "sit." She obeyed immediately. Nicholls and the vicar stepped inside the small, yet neatly organised shop and walked up to the counter at the far end. Mr. Malik saw them approach. He stiffened as he always did in the presence of authority.

"Good afternoon sirs! And madams!" he said, in his heavily accented English.

"Hello, Mr. Malik." Annabelle beamed.

"Have you heard from your son, yet?" Inspector Nicholls inquired, brooking no small talk and remembering vividly the difficulties they had had in their previous interview. He and Mr. Malik had struggled to understand one another. The shopkeeper shrugged and spread his hands wide.

"Aziz not here. Always busy. School. Study. Exercise with bike. Visit with friends. Work with cars. I told you."

"Aren't you worried?" Annabelle asked. "Aziz has not been seen for two days!"

Mr. Malik smiled widely and laughed. "Aziz is good boy! When he finish with everything, then he come, eat, go out again."

"But it's dangerous. There's been a murder, Mr. Malik.

Aziz should be home now!"

Mr. Malik wagged his finger furiously. "No, no, no, no! Aziz not dangerous. Never. Very soft boy. Kind."

"No, you don't understand," Annabelle said, her tone growing ever-so-slightly urgent. "It's dangerous *for* Aziz."

"No," the bearded shopkeeper repeated adamantly. "Seventeen years, no trouble. Teachers say perfect student. Go to Oxford. Very good to parents. Aziz not trouble, dangerous, nothing."

Annabelle exchanged a defeated look with the inspector who opened his mouth to speak, frustration clear on his face. Sensing that his involvement in the exchange wasn't going to move the situation forward, Annabelle quickly pressed a hand to the inspector's elbow. It seemed to do the trick. All Nicholls emitted was a deep sigh.

"We'll be back, Mr. Malik," he said.

"Thank you," Annabelle added.

"Anytime!" the shopkeeper called heartily.

Annabelle and the inspector walked outside, reclaimed the puppy, and took a few steps down the street before stopping. The inspector shook his head angrily. "Do you see what I'm dealing with, Reverend? I've called for a translator to come from Truro, but they won't be here until tomorrow at the earliest. By then, it could be too late."

Annabelle gazed around the street as if an answer might drive by at any moment. When she turned back to the inspector, she noticed a movement in the driveway beside Mr. Malik's corner shop. She watched as a tall, slim, strikingly beautiful young woman slowly eased herself out of the shop's rear entrance. Nicholls turned to look at who had caught Annabelle's eye.

The woman closed the shop door silently behind her. "Officer!" she hissed as she walked quickly over. "Officer!"

CHAPTER NINETEEN

THE YOUNG WOMAN looked to be in her late teens or early twenties. She had a pair of intelligent brown eyes, smooth, light-brown skin, and full lips. Her hair fell thick and lustrous about her shoulders. It swayed dramatically in the breeze. "My name is Samira Malik. I'm Aziz's sister."

Annabelle squinted at her for barely a second. "I know you."

"Yes," the girl smiled. "And I remember you, too. I met you at the village craft fair this summer. It's nice to see you again, Reverend Dixon."

They shook hands and smiled at each other before a cloud of doubt crossed Annabelle's face. "But I've not seen you since then . . . Where have you been?"

Samira nodded. "I'm at Brighton University. I'm only here for the weekend, though I didn't know all *this* would happen."

"All *this?*" the inspector asked.

Samira scanned the street before slowly backing up into the shadows. She beckoned to Annabelle and Nicholls.

They exchanged a glance before following her. Once they were huddled into the tight space between the small car in the driveway and the front of the garage next to the shop, Samira leant forwards and spoke quietly, conspiring with them.

"Aziz *is* missing!" she said.

"What!" Annabelle cried loudly before covering her mouth. "What?" she repeated, much more quietly.

"Aziz should have come home over twenty-four hours ago, and my father knows that. He's desperate to find him, even more than you."

"So let's go and speak to him," Nicholls insisted gruffly. "Surely you can communicate with him. Tell him that we're looking for Aziz, that he might be in danger, and anything he tells us will—"

"No," Samira interrupted, shaking her head gravely. "That won't work. I heard you talking. My father is only pretending not to understand. You see, my dad thinks that Aziz has found a girlfriend. It's his biggest fear. Ever since Aziz was ten years old, my father has worried that he would find some unsuitable girl with whom he would run away. He's not telling you this because he's ashamed. Of all the plans my father has for Aziz, marrying a nice Pakistani girl is the most important to him."

"Well, isn't it possible?" the inspector said, as he tugged the puppy to him to stop her from exploring. "Could Aziz have run off with a girl?"

Samira shook her head firmly. "No. Aziz already gets plenty of attention from girls. His mind is purely on his studies and doing things the right way—in that sense, he's like my father."

"Seems possible to me. A teenage boy who isn't interested in girls?" the inspector said, bending down to scratch the puppy's ears and stop her gentle whining. "That's all I thought about when I was his age." Annabelle frowned at the inspector, but he was too preoccupied with the dog to notice.

"If he did run off, I would be the first to know," Samira said. "We tell each other everything. That's why I'm so worried—"

Samira turned her head sharply as she heard her father's voice call out from inside the shop. He was merely having a simple exchange with a customer but unsettled by the sound, Samira retreated further into the shadow of the shuttered garage. She kept her voice low as she leant over again to speak.

"I've not heard anything from Aziz since Friday morning."

"The day before yesterday."

"Yes. Not a call or a text. Nothing. And I've been sending him messages all weekend. He knew I was visiting. We're very close. There's no way he's alright and hasn't thought to message me back or come to see me. No way."

They were quiet for a moment as they reflected on what this might mean. Suddenly, their thoughts were interrupted by the sound of clattering metal as the puppy leapt at the garage shutters, clawing at them roughly with her front paws.

"Hey!" called the inspector, pulling the pup back.

The puppy strained at her lead with every ounce of her strength, whining and barking. Annabelle kneeled down and tried to placate her but she remained intent on the metal garage doors, her paws scrabbling at the air in desperation.

The rear door to the shop opened suddenly, and Samira's eyes seemed to double in size. Her father appeared shouting angrily at what he thought were intruders or local boys intent on trouble before his rage was replaced by confusion at the sight that greeted him.

"What's going on?" he said, his eyes flicking rapidly between the three figures and a singular, small, yet loud and agitated puppy. After the elder Malik exchanged some quick, tense words with Samira in their native language, the inspector broke into their conversation.

"What have you got in here?" he said. He held the dog's lead with both hands to stop the puppy from throwing herself against the doors again.

"Nothing!" Mr. Malik cried with a big shrug. "Delivery tonight. I not open since Friday!"

"Well, open it now!" Nicholls ordered in a voice he usually saved for his officers. Annabelle winced.

Mr. Malik looked hard at the inspector but quickly took a ring of keys from his pocket and walked over to the metal shutter. He went to unlock the padlock, but when he got close, he found it hanging. Frowning, Malik set the lock aside and lifted the wide shutter with the help of his knee.

It flew up with a heavy clank. The "thunk" as it rolled back echoed in a split-second of silence. As the echo reverberated, Annabelle, Samira, and the inspector briefly anticipated what they might find before the scene exploded in a blur of cries, shouts, and frenzied activity.

First, the puppy lunged at the garage interior. The inspector was taken by surprise, the lead flew out of his hands. The dog bounded down the side of the minivan parked inside. She aimed for the back of the garage, quickly followed by Samira, who screamed loudly. Then, with his hands on his head and a series of cries in Urdu, Mr. Malik did the same.

Annabelle and the inspector followed only a step

behind, but by the time they reached the source of everyone's panic, the scene at the back of the garage was frantic. Laments in foreign tongues, the puppy's furious barking, and Samira's long cries of horror and despair cut through the wintery, cold air.

There, in the corner at the back of the garage was Aziz. And he was not in good shape. He had been badly beaten.

Aziz was shivering. He lay curled in a foetal position. Black, crusted blood stained half his face. He clutched his right forearm to his body, his chin tucked defensively. His eyes were closed, his clothes ripped and covered in dark stains. Blue bruises streaked his legs and torso.

After stretching out to touch her brother but pulling back when she realised she might hurt him further, Samira couldn't bear to look anymore. She stood up and turned away, her usually pretty face smeared with the ugliness of utter desolation. Annabelle opened her arms and the young woman fell into them, clutching the vicar tightly as she wailed.

"I've called an ambulance," Nicholls shouted.

"We'll meet you at the hospital," Annabelle shouted back, as she cajoled the sobbing girl away from the scene, the puppy trailing in her wake.

CHAPTER TWENTY

NICHOLLS RODE WITH Mr. Malik and Aziz in the ambulance. In hot pursuit were Annabelle, Samira, and the puppy. In her Mini Cooper, Annabelle glanced over and talked persistently to soothe the traumatised and now dumbstruck girl.

On reaching the hospital, Nicholls pulled Mr. Malik aside before he entered the building, knowing full well that the dazed, shocked man was too shaken to communicate in anything other than his native tongue and would only get in the way of the emergency medical team. Acting in silent partnership, Annabelle followed the paramedics as they pulled Aziz out of the vehicle and took him quickly inside. With her arm around Samira's shoulders, Annabelle waited for ten minutes whilst the doctors looked Aziz over and then listened closely to their assessment. Eventually, Mr. Malik joined them, and Annabelle left so that Samira could communicate the doctor's words to her father. The vicar met the inspector outside. He had taken the puppy from Annabelle's car and was kneeling down to feed her some treats he had saved in his coat pocket.

"What did the doctors say?" Nicholls asked, standing up as Annabelle walked towards him looking troubled.

She sighed and shook her head at the brutality of Aziz's attack. "He's going to be alright, but it will take time. He's not only been beaten, but he's in shock now. It looks like he's been lying in the corner of the garage since yesterday."

"When can I speak to him?"

"The doctor said he'll need at least twenty-four hours before he can talk to anyone. I don't understand. Why was he just lying there? His family was next door. Why would he suffer like that instead of going home?"

Nicholls stared into the distance. "It's not so strange. Stupid, yes, but not uncommon. I see it a lot with young lads, tough ones especially. When they get beaten up like that, their first reaction is rarely to get help or tell someone. Their pride tends to hurt twice as much as their injuries. They worry more about what their peers will think when they find out, or in Aziz's case, his family."

"Surely not!"

"You'd be surprised, Reverend. Aziz's father seems to worship the boy for being spotless, a hard worker, and never in any trouble. Aziz doesn't even fool around with girls because his father doesn't want him to. The kid's probably deeply ashamed that this happened to him."

"It's such nonsense," Annabelle said, though she understood the inspector was probably right. "I'll never understand men and their 'manly pride!'"

Nicholls gave the vicar a rueful smile before turning back to her car. "Do you mind giving us a lift back to the station, Reverend?"

"Of course not," Annabelle said and began getting in the driver's seat as the inspector urged the puppy into the back.

"You know," Nicholls said, as he eased himself into his seat, his head grazing the roof of the small car, "I think patience is the only tool, pardon the pun, I have left to throw at this case."

Annabelle smiled sadly. "I understand, Inspector. But it was only yesterday that the murder happened. You're not giving yourself much time."

"True," the inspector said, looking over at the back seat to check on his dog as they drove along. "Still, this is one of those cases where progress doesn't just seem slow, it seems to be going backwards."

"Surely it's not that bad," Annabelle said. She deftly shifted gear.

"I'm afraid it is," the inspector sighed.

"Can I help?"

"No, I don't think so. I mean no disrespect, Reverend, I admire your faith in people, but I believe it's a faith that's sometimes afforded to those who don't deserve it."

"What do you mean, Inspector?" Annabelle said, pouting.

"Well, take Ted Lovesey. Lovesey maintains he was gambling at the time of the murder, but he can't talk about it nor provide anyone to alibi him. Very convenient. To me, he looks suspicious as hell, but you believe he's innocent. I was willing to countenance the idea, but now our only other suspect has just turned up in no state to talk and is more likely a victim than a murderer. Consequently, the spotlight of suspicion falls back onto Lovesey."

"I don't think Ted Lovesey murdered Mildred, Inspector!"

"I know you don't. But that's not rational, logical, you see? In short, I'm saying that I think your openness and generosity, your belief in people is naïve and sometimes misplaced."

"Inspector!" Annabelle exclaimed.

"Now calm down, Reverend," Nicholls continued in his commanding voice. "Ted may not be the murderer. And I'm not trying to insult you, I'm telling you this for your own good. I don't actually think we're dealing with your typical parishioner in this case. Aziz took a severe beating, and Mildred's murder was brutal. A very dangerous person or persons are behind this. Criminals, murderers, psychopaths. And they're as good at lying as they are at committing crimes. A little bit of scepticism wouldn't do you any harm, Reverend. You need to be careful."

Annabelle gripped the wheel tightly and focused on parking the car, angered by the inspector's criticism but unable to call on sufficient evidence to dismiss it entirely.

"What will you do with Ted?" she asked, pulling at the handbrake with more force than was necessary. Nicholls shrugged.

"I'll release him for now. We've got his prints, but we don't have the evidence to detain him further. Besides, if we get a match on the fuel can or the murder weapon, I doubt we'll have trouble finding him again. He doesn't seem like the smartest tool in the box."

"I'll come in with you," Annabelle announced, unclipping her seatbelt. "I'm sure Ted would appreciate a lift after this ordeal."

They entered the police station together, the dog once more cheerfully padding along between them, although there was no mistaking the vicar and the inspector for a happy couple this time.

As soon as Inspector Nicholls entered the reception area, Constable McAllister bounced up from her chair and made a beeline for him. Constables Harris and Raven watched her from behind their desks.

"Inspector!" she said.

"What is it, McAllister?"

"Well, there's good news and bad news," she said, flicking a glance at Annabelle without moving her head. "Two bits of bad news, perhaps?"

"Go on," Nicholls urged.

"The bad news is that there were no prints on the fuel can. Either they were washed away by the rain, or the person who used it didn't leave any."

"Damnit. What's the good news?"

"Harper will give us the results of her tests on the murder weapon shortly," she added uncertainly, obviously fearful of what the inspector might say about this delay. "It's taking longer than she thought."

As it turned out, the inspector didn't react much. He looked from the young constable to Annabelle, then back again. "I really hope Harper comes through for us. We need a breakthrough."

Despite their earlier disagreement, Annabelle found herself placing a sympathetic hand on the inspector's arm at the sight of his downcast face.

"We may not agree on some things, Inspector, but I have a feeling we are closer to finding the person who did this than we think."

"Are you ever less than utterly optimistic, Reverend?"

"Golly gosh, Inspector. I hope not."

CHAPTER TWENTY-ONE

ANNABELLE'S THOUGHTS WERE so turbulent and confused that she muttered to herself as she drove, completely forgetting that Ted was sitting beside her in the passenger seat. Already uneasy from spending hours in the interview room, Ted glanced at the reverend nervously but decided against saying anything. When it became clear, however, that the vicar was heading towards the church and not, in fact, his own home, he found himself with no choice but to speak up.

"Um . . . Vicar?"

"Oh!" Annabelle exclaimed, swivelling her head, startled to find Ted beside her. "Yes?"

"I think you missed the turn. My house is down that way."

"Oh!" Annabelle repeated. "Sorry."

She looked out of the side window and wondered when the next opportunity to make a U-turn would be. Then she reconsidered.

"Actually, would you like to stop by my cottage and have a cup of tea, Ted? I could give you a lift home later. I'm sure we could both do with some company considering what has happened."

Ted took a moment to think about the offer. He lived alone, had little money, and now that Mildred was dead, he had no job. He had nothing to do but sit at home or go down the pub where he was likely to spend what little money he did have on drink.

"That sounds alright, actually. Thanks, Vicar."

Annabelle smiled as she eased the car into the church driveway. Her cottage looked warm and inviting on this cold winter's evening. A moment later, they went inside and made their way to the kitchen.

"Hello, Reverend," Philippa said, her back to them as she pulled a tray out of the oven. She turned around and opened her eyes wide. "Oh, hello, Ted."

"Hi, Philippa," he said meekly.

"Would you put the kettle on, Philippa? I need a cup of tea and a slice of cake even more desperately than usual." Philippa obliged as the reverend and the mechanic sat at the kitchen table.

"How are you feeling, Ted?" Annabelle said as she foraged in her pockets.

Ted sighed. "Stunned. I haven't had a moment to think, let alone feel anything. One minute I'm being dragged out of Greg's house, the next I hear about Mildred, then I'm being treated like I'm the one who killed her! It's not like I was having the best weekend as it was, what with—"

Ted stopped himself abruptly. Annabelle understood perfectly. Ted had struggled to tell *her* about the gambling ring. He wasn't about to start spilling the beans with another person in the room, especially when that person was a village gossip extraordinaire. Annabelle stood up and walked over to her church secretary.

"I'll make the tea, Philippa. You go sit down."

Annabelle poured a little water into the teapot and let it warm as she set the tray with cups, sugar, teaspoons, and milk. After she'd added the tea leaves and filled the pot with boiling water, she turned back to the table. She set the teapot down before walking over to open a large square biscuit tin sat on the counter.

"What's this?" Annabelle asked Philippa, looking inside the tin.

"What? Oh, Mrs. Clunes left those for you. She'd made too many and thought you might like a few."

"Well, she was right!" Annabelle exclaimed as she looked over the half-dozen dainty madeleines in the tin. Annabelle placed the coconut-covered pink spongy confections onto a plate and went to sit back down with the others.

"Oh!" Philippa exclaimed suddenly. She stood up. "I'll go and get Jeremy. The poor boy's been weeding the cemetery all afternoon. I'm sure he'd love a cup of tea too."

"Good idea," Annabelle said through a mouthful of cake.

Annabelle watched Philippa leave, then looked back at Ted. He smiled awkwardly as he took a slow sip of his tea, seeming to take some courage from the hot brew.

"Thanks, Vicar," he said softly. "For everything."

"Oh, tosh!" Annabelle smiled, gently placing her cup down. "I know you didn't do it, Ted. You've got nothing to worry about. You've no need to act so apologetic."

"Well, I'm not entirely innocent," he said. Annabelle raised an eyebrow. "The gambling," he added in a whisper.

"Oh, yes."

"Look, Vicar, please don't tell anybody about that. If it got out that I'd—"

"Of course I won't, Ted. But you really should tell

someone about it. Or at the very least get yourself away from such things. No good can come of it."

Ted put his cup down heavily as if lacking even the energy to hold it. "I know, Vicar." He gazed at the table for a few moments.

"What exactly *is* this gambling ring? How did it work?" Annabelle asked, hoping to disrupt his mood.

Ted looked up with frightened eyes. "If I tell you, you can't tell no one, right? Doctor-patient confidentiality, or . . . or like a confession? Something like that?"

Annabelle chuckled lightly. "Well, I'm not a doctor, and confession is for Catholics. But I can promise you, I'm a woman of my word, and I won't say anything to anyone."

Ted's shoulders settled, and he breathed deeply. He began to tell his tale.

"It began as an innocent poker night. Just a few of the men getting together for the fun of it. They didn't even play for money, to begin with. It was just a way for some of the men to relax. Upton St. Mary's a small place, so any chance to do something new or go somewhere different is welcome."

"Where did you play?"

"Various places. Someone's barn one week, an empty school the next. Whoever joined in would offer a place to play. That was part of the fun, I think: the whispers of where it would be next, trying to find out, getting an invitation, but keeping it all a secret. Only certain people could join. It was quite an honour. It was like a secret gentlemen's club."

"Sounds like a boy's club to me," Annabelle said, rolling her eyes.

"Not for long," Ted answered. "At first, it was just a few of the guys, the ones with the . . . er . . . most 'difficult' wives

". . . It was their chance to get away for a bit. I was never a regular. I only went a few times, and only once on a Friday, but the rest of us kept it a secret because we knew how much those men appreciated the chance to just disappear for a few hours. It was exciting. But then things changed."

"What?"

"I don't really know how it happened exactly, but outsiders started coming. Men, dangerous men, from other places. It was perfect for them. Hidden locations, a system for inviting people anonymously. In the bigger cities, the police are always watching them and know all the places where these kinds of things are held. But no copper would think to look for a high-rolling gambling ring in Upton St. Mary. It was perfect because it was so unlikely."

Annabelle sat back and shook her head at the sheer lunacy of it all. "Weren't the outside men a little out of your league? Why did the Upton St. Mary men continue to play?"

"They had to!" Ted said emphatically. "For one thing, the local boys knew the area. They were the ones providing the locations. Without them spreading the word and arranging it all, the outsiders wouldn't have been able to play. And these men, they just . . . well, they didn't *do* anything exactly, they just *felt* evil. A look. Or a walk, you know? And who knew what these . . . *criminals* would do if someone stopped turning up to the tables? Or the tables stopped happening? These men were not nice people, Vicar. I'm not saying nobody was enticed by winning big. These guys brought a lot of money to the table, but the vast majority of men who were taking part, in the end, did so out of fear, not greed, in my opinion."

"And what was the reason in your case, Ted?" Annabelle asked, gently.

Ted smiled weakly. "You can probably guess, Vicar. I might have been afraid of those men, but I'm even more afraid of not having any money. I'm a forty-six-year-old mechanic. I live by himself and spend all my money on booze. The opportunity to win the amounts being thrown around at those games—and they were pretty big, let me tell you—was just too much for me to resist."

"You sound quite self-aware, though."

"Hours locked up in a police station will do that to you," Ted said. Annabelle smirked sympathetically. "The only thing that keeps me going is the dream of hitting it big somehow, and with this gambling . . . I don't know. I suppose I thought I was due a bit of luck."

"But you lost everything, didn't you, Ted?"

"How did you know?"

"You didn't go home. You went to Greg's on Saturday morning. Were you scared? Do you owe those men money, now?"

Ted took his tea with shaky hands, lifted it to his lips, and gulped.

CHAPTER TWENTY-TWO

"WE'RE BACK!" PHILIPPA'S sing-songy voice cried out as she came through the front door. She slammed it shut with a bang. "Took forever to find him! I thought the ground had finally caved in and swallowed him up! But he was just behind that big tombstone at the back." She walked into the kitchen, followed by Jeremy, who gently pulled off a pair of large, rough gardening gloves.

"Oh, Jeremy, you shouldn't be weeding. What about those lovely musician's hands of yours?" Annabelle laughed.

Jeremy smiled mildly. "It's quite alright, Reverend."

"Ted," Annabelle said, "this is Jeremy. Our church organist."

"Pleased to meet you," Jeremy said, offering his long fingers.

Ted took his hand and shook it. He squinted at Jeremy. "Likewise . . . Have we met before?"

Jeremy's smile vanished. "I don't think so," he said.

"I could swear I've seen you recently," Ted replied.

"Ted's one of the mechanics over at Mildred's," Philippa chipped in helpfully.

"Ah," Jeremy said. "I brought my car in for a service a while back. That must be it."

"Yeah," Ted replied, unsure. "Maybe."

"Anyway," Philippa said, flapping the introductions away and pulling out a seat from the table, "sit yourself down and have a cup of tea, Jeremy. You must be freezing."

"Actually," Jeremy said, his eyes darting between the three of them, "I really should get going. I don't feel too well. My grandmother will be waiting."

"Oh, poppycock!" Annabelle said. "I'm sure you can spare a few minutes for a cup of tea!"

But Jeremy was already halfway to the door when he called back. "I'll see you tomorrow, Vicar. Bye, Philippa!"

"Jeremy!" Philippa called out hopelessly before she heard the front door close. She turned to Annabelle with a bemused look.

"He's certainly a strange one, isn't he?" Annabelle said.

"But lovably so," Philippa smiled as she sat at the table.

They chattered on for a few more minutes as they finished their teas. Graciously, Annabelle steered the talk away from the bizarre, tragic events of the weekend, but Ted's morose state cast a dark cloud over the conversation.

Once he was done with his tea, Annabelle offered to drive Ted home. He accepted gratefully. It was a short trip, one that the mechanic could easily have walked, yet Annabelle understood his reasons for wishing to spend a few more minutes in her company. Anything to stave off the desolate, fearful loneliness that awaited him at home.

"Do you have any plans now, Ted?" Annabelle said as she steered her car around a corner. "Perhaps it would be nice to get away for a little while. Do you have any family outside the village?"

She kept her eyes on the road, but when Ted failed to respond, she glanced over and noticed him looking down at the floor. "Ted?"

"Yes?" he said, startled.

Annabelle frowned at him. "Is everything alright?"

Ted opened his mouth, closed it again, gazed forwards, then back to his lap. He was indecisive, she'd give him that.

"Ted . . . ?" Annabelle repeated. She could see something was very much on his mind and that he was wrestling over whether to share it with her.

"I . . . I shouldn't really say this," Ted began slowly. "But I suppose I owe you."

He paused for a long time. Annabelle parked the car easily in front of his house, stopped the engine, and turned to him.

"I promise I won't tell anyone if that's what you want," she said.

Ted smiled shyly. "I know you won't. I don't even know if this is important. But I just thought you might want to know. You seem quite close . . ."

"Close? What are you talking about, Ted?"

"That man at your cottage."

Annabelle took a second to think. "Jeremy?"

"Yes. I know exactly where I've seen him before. And I'm fairly certain he remembers me, judging by the way he left in such a hurry."

"Surely not," Annabelle said as the realisation dawned on her. "You must be mistaken. Jeremy would never engage in those gambling games!"

Ted snorted and shook his head. "He's pretty recognisable. Not the kind of man you can really mistake. He was a regular. I never went to a game where he *wasn't* there."

Annabelle sat back in the driver's seat as if pinned to it. "I don't believe it . . ."

"I told you. The ring is much bigger than it looks."

Annabelle spoke defiantly. "He must have been one of those men trapped in the ring, as you said. Perhaps he went once, out of curiosity, and kept going because of fear."

Ted shook his head again. "No, it wasn't that," he said. "That's why I wanted to tell you. That guy—Jeremy—he was one of the biggest gamblers at the games. Loved it, he did. But he's in trouble now. I owe them a lot, that's why I'm afraid to go home." Ted glanced sadly at his front door. "But *him*, he owes them even more."

Annabelle put her hands on the wheel and clenched it tightly as if steadying herself against a hurricane. She couldn't believe what she was hearing.

"Be careful, Reverend," Ted said, finally. He opened the door and got out. Before walking away, he leant in to add, "And thank you again."

Annabelle felt a pang as Ted returned to his unlit, empty home, the street seeming even darker than usual for this time of night. She made a silent promise to check up on him first thing the next morning and sped off, still digesting the utterly fantastical idea that her church organist was a gambler.

When she got back to the church and got out of her car, Annabelle heard the loud, throbbing notes of the church organ filter through the air. The churchyard was lit only by the two lamp posts at its gate, the gentle glow through the church's stained-glass windows, and the warm orange light that emerged from behind the curtains of her cottage. She locked the Mini and looked over to where Philippa was closing the front door behind her, still fiddling with her coat buttons.

"Are you going home, Philippa?" Annabelle asked as they met on the short path that led to her doorstep.

"Yes," Philippa answered, reaching around the back of her neck to find the end of her scarf. "The puppy's just fallen asleep, so I'm taking my chance whilst I can! He tends to follow me otherwise, and I have a terrible time getting him back in the house!"

Annabelle smiled and helped Philippa find the end of her scarf, bringing it around the front so she could tie it. "That's because you're just as attached to him as he is to you."

Philippa chuckled. "Who wouldn't be? And how is the other little one? Has the inspector fallen for her charms yet?"

"I believe so," Annabelle said. "She's terribly inquisitive. The perfect companion for a detective." The two women turned to the church as a loud swell of chords rose into the night sky.

"I hear Jeremy's at it again. That boy has such dedication." Philippa shook her head in wonderment.

"Indeed," Annabelle murmured.

"Well, I'll be off then, Vicar."

"Good night, Philippa."

Annabelle pottered over to her cottage and went inside. The moment she shut the door behind her, she felt a wave of exhaustion come over her. She had been buzzing around all day, performing the service in the morning, enduring the ordeal of discovering Aziz in the afternoon, and piecing together the story of the gambling ring.

The emotional toll had been even greater. Although Mildred's murder had occurred only a day ago, it felt like a lifetime since she last experienced an innocent thought about something trivial. She had dedicated almost every ounce of her energy to discovering the truth and when she walked into her kitchen, she realised her reserves were in short supply.

She went straight for the meringues that Philippa had baked for her. Her church secretary usually made her something sweet on Sundays, a sort of post-service treat. It was essential for Annabelle to always have a supply of sweets on hand. She needed an emergency stash to give her fortitude during those times she desperately needed it. This was one of those times.

The sight of the meringues perked Annabelle up no end, sandwiched as they were with thick, whipped, fresh Cornish cream, quite possibly made from the milk of one of those cows belonging to Leo Tremethick that had held her up the day before. She took a plate, placed some of the meringues on it and made her way to the living room couch. She flopped down and smiled at the sweet-smelling treats. As if by magic, Biscuit appeared around the door.

"Hello, Biscuit. To what do I owe this pleasure?"

Annabelle scoffed one of the meringues in seconds, then slowed down to savour the taste of another more fully. A few deliberate chews into the third, and she found her sweet tooth finally satisfied. Biscuit, who had been circling her ankles, deftly jumped onto the arm of her chair and went to sniff the plate, no doubt planning to finish what Annabelle had left behind. Annabelle quickly whisked the meringue out of the cat's reach and gathered her up, placating her with vigorous strokes that the ginger tabby tolerated with an air of resignation as if she were doing Annabelle a favour. In her sugary haze, Annabelle's thoughts slowly turned to the conundrums that had bothered her since finding Mildred's body.

"I need to go to bed, Biscuit. Time for me to rest my weary head. Whittling and worrying won't help anyone." Annabelle started to rise from her chair before immediately falling back into it. "But this news about Jeremy being a gambler is shocking! What would his grandmother say? I'm sure she would be horrified."

Biscuit indicated her disinterest in Jeremy's money and nana problems by yawning and wriggling out of Annabelle's arms. The cat settled on the cushion beside her owner as a few short, sharp, stabbing high notes drew Annabelle's attention to the window.

"There he is again. Playing as though nothing has happened. What do you think goes through his mind, eh, Biscuit?"

Usually, Annabelle could hear Jeremy playing the organ only faintly but this time, the silence of her empty cottage and the lateness of the hour made it so that the sound pierced the air. Annabelle felt a shiver run down her spine. It seemed she had a front-row seat at a performance as Jeremy proceeded into a fast, manic, complex Bach concerto. The combination of powerful, dark music, the blackness of the night, and her many unanswered questions made her mind rush.

"*Jeremy?*" she said quietly to herself, finding her idea almost too implausible to speak out loud. "Surely not."

CHAPTER TWENTY-THREE

ANNABELLE STARED OUT of the window into a scene that now seemed entirely frightening. The twisted, leafless branches of the trees cast imposing outlines against the night sky. A round moon hid behind black clouds as if afraid. Leaves swirled in the courtyard.

To the strains of Bach's genius, Annabelle's thoughts raced so far ahead that she could barely catch them. She shook her head and continued to talk to Biscuit as she ran her hands one after the other from the baby-soft fur between the ginger tabby's ears to her tail in an attempt to calm her nerves.

"It's one thing for Ted to be involved, Biscuit. It seems perfectly natural for a man with such an addictive personality. It's even reasonable to think that many of the men in the village would indulge themselves in a spot of gambling now and again. Upton St. Mary is a wonderful, interesting, and accommodating place, but it does lack an element of danger and excitement. A clandestine game of cards would seem rather appealing to many men, I imagine. But Jeremy is different. He's not like many men. He is pure and good. He tells me so."

Annabelle rubbed the underside of Biscuit's chin. Now, not even Biscuit could hide her pleasure. The cat stretched her neck upwards and closed her eyes in ecstasy.

"So what else might he be hiding?"

Annabelle recalled her conversations with Jeremy, searching them for clues to his secret life as a gambler. Nowhere, not even in his regularly odd or awkward behaviour, could she find evidence of subterfuge—and this worried her more than anything.

Still watching the church through the kitchen window, she noticed Jeremy's car. It was an old Toyota that he always parked snugly in the shadow of the trees.

"You know, Biscuit, I wonder if Jeremy was telling the truth when he gave me the message about my car being ready, when he said he'd met Ian Crawford in the village. Whilst I have a hard time suspecting Jeremy of duplicity, I have no such struggle when it comes to Ian Crawford. Far be it for me to cast aspersions, he that is without sin and all that, but perhaps they are fellow gamblers!" Annabelle went to her desk and began scanning her bulging phonebook for a number before furiously dialling.

"Hello?" came a subdued, tremulous voice on the other end.

"Ted! It's Reverend Annabelle."

"Oh. I'm alright, Reverend," Ted said, his voice loosening into a gentle chuckle. "You don't have to check up on me every five minutes, though the thought is much appreciated."

"Oh, that's not why I'm calling," Annabelle said. "But

I'm glad you're okay. Actually, I wanted to ask you something... About what we talked about earlier."

"Yes?" Ted said, his voice tightening again.

"When you were here, Jeremy said he'd brought his car in for servicing. Was that true? Or were you just covering up for each other?" There was a slight pause.

"Oh," Ted exclaimed as he remembered. "Yeah, he actually did bring it by. A Toyota Corolla."

Annabelle looked outside at Jeremy's car. "Yes. That's it."

"I didn't work on it though, Mildred did. She and his grandmother go way back, or something like that. So I can't tell you what was wrong with it. Sorry."

"That's all I wanted to know. Thanks, Ted."

"Anytime," he replied, as they both hung up.

Annabelle returned to the window, the sound of the music seeming to swell as it passed through the trees. It was even louder now. Something was very wrong. She could see how these things were easily explainable coincidences—Jeremy's visit to Mildred, his bumping into Ian Crawford, his appearance at the gambling games—but Annabelle's instincts were fired-up now, and they were telling her that something was going on. She had overlooked Jeremy. As a church organist, a close friend, and a valued member of her parish, he had been in her blind spot, but now that Annabelle focused on him, her doubts surfaced.

"Come now, Annabelle," she told herself as she turned away from the window, "you're just getting paranoid and impatient. A good night's rest is what you need."

Just as she was about to walk upstairs, the phone startled her by ringing loudly. She jumped, then laughed away her surprise as she placed a palm over her heart. Still smiling, she picked up the receiver.

"Hello?"

"Hello, Reverend."

"Inspector! How are you?"

"Confused but persistent, as always, Reverend."

"Is there something I can help you with?"

"There is," Nicholls said. "I just heard from Harper. Her report on the murder weapon. A wrench. No clear fingerprints, but she did say that the hand that wielded the wrench was unusually large. The thing is, we don't record hand sizes in public records."

Annabelle laughed. "I suppose we should start measuring hands then! We could start with the musicians. Our church organist has—" She stopped suddenly, her smile fading as terror, confusion, and shock transformed her.

"Reverend?" the inspector prompted after moments of silence.

"Yes," Annabelle replied slowly.

"You were saying something?"

Annabelle's mouth suddenly felt impossibly dry. She realised that her heart was racing. She held her breath and her eyes flickered in the direction of the church. Usually, Annabelle had plenty of time to think things through, and she enjoyed reaching decisions carefully and deliberately. At this moment, however, she realised that she had mere seconds to decide whether to reveal what she knew to the inspector, thereby incriminating a man she would not have suspected of even a minor crime just minutes ago.

"Reverend?" Nicholls repeated, quicker this time. "Is everything alright?"

"Inspector," she said, "would you mind dropping by so we can go over something?"

"Now?" he replied. "I could come by after I've gone

through some reports. Say about half an hour? Unless it's urgent?"

"No, it's not," Annabelle replied, narrowing her eyes as she looked in the direction of the church.

CHAPTER TWENTY-FOUR

JEREMY WAS STILL playing furiously when Annabelle left her cottage. The powerful, vibrating notes of the organ intermingled with the wind that whistled through the empty branches and rustled the dry leaves on the ground, creating a wall of bone-shudderingly eerie sounds. The temperature had dropped, and the night sky was a shade of deep, velvety black.

Annabelle's beloved church had never seemed so ominous or imposing to her as it did now. The elegant gothic structure reached into the dark sky, the stained glass windows glowing with shadowy, opaque light. Suddenly, she understood why the children of the village had concocted stories about the cemetery at night.

"Come now, Annabelle," she told herself. "There's nothing to worry about. It's just Jeremy, and it's just a particularly dark and chilly night."

With a sense of purpose that was only a little stronger than the fear in her heart, Annabelle walked to the church. The sounds of her tentative feet on the gravel were barely audible above the increasing volume of the organ. She reached the big double doors at the church's entrance and pushed through them into the nave.

Once again, Annabelle was struck by how different St. Mary's seemed at night. The low-wattage lamps on the pillars amidst the pews as well as those on the walls gave off a dim, flickering, yellow light. They allowed plenty of shadows to play around the church's nooks, corners, and crannies. Perhaps it was the music, she thought, that made everything appear so sombre and dramatic.

The sounds vibrated around the high walls of the centuries-old church, the hard, cold stone refusing to absorb the tones, the notes pulsating in her ears. Annabelle's stomach turned over. She felt that she was in a scene from an old black and white horror movie. She shivered as she made her way up the aisle. As she approached the hunched figure of Jeremy, sitting with his back to her over the keyboard of the vast organ, she steeled herself.

"Jeremy!" she called. Her voice shook. "Jeremy!"

The tall, young man continued to play, engrossed in the music and the almost superhuman dexterity of his long fingers. Annabelle brought herself to within ten paces of the steps that led up to the altar. She slowed to a stop.

"Jeremy!" she called once again but still there was no response. She took a deep breath and walked closer until she was within a few feet of him, close enough to see the stitches in the pattern of his dark-blue cardigan.

"Jere—"

With a dissonant clang of a minor chord, the organist stopped playing. He spun around. Annabelle jumped back, one hand to her chest, the other out in front of her.

"Oh!" cried Jeremy, allowing himself to relax. "You startled me, Vicar!"

Annabelle smiled and took a moment to exhale. "And you startled me!"

"I apologise," Jeremy said, bowing his head. "I was completely absorbed in my playing."

"Yes, I could tell."

"Am I bothering you? Is that what you came to tell me?" he said, checking his watch. "I suppose it is rather late."

"Actually," Annabelle began. She took a few steps forwards. She felt calmer now. The music had stopped, and Jeremy's easy manner was relaxing her a little. "I wanted to speak to you about something else. Something rather serious."

Jeremy raised an eyebrow curiously and shifted around on his stool to face the reverend fully. Annabelle clasped her hands together tightly and gazed down at them as she considered how to begin. She had promised Ted that she would not mention what he had told her about Jeremy's gambling. She needed to be tactful and, if her deepest suspicions were correct, careful.

"How is your grandmother faring?"

"Quite well, Vicar. Of course, she doesn't get out much these days, but the villagers are very kind to visit her. She's not short of company."

"How did she take the news of Mildred's death? I understand they were close."

Jeremy's smile remained on his face, his eyes dark in the gloom. "They'd known each other a long time but my grandmother hadn't seen her for a while. Mildred was not one of her regular visitors. Too busy with her business, I expect."

Annabelle smiled back. "Did you happen to know Mildred yourself?"

Jeremy smiled easily. "A little. My car breaks down rather a lot. It's old. I should get a new one."

Annabelle nodded. "Perhaps Ian Crawford would sell you one. He deals in used cars." Jeremy stared at Annabelle, saying nothing. "Do you happen to know anything about a gambling ring, Jeremy? One that some of the men in Upton St. Mary have become involved in? Maybe Ian Crawford, too?"

Jeremy shook his head and frowned. "Vicar! I am surprised you see fit to question me about such things!" He paused for a second. "Did that mechanic say anything to you when he was at your cottage earlier?"

"Ted? No. Why would you think that?"

Jeremy was flustered for a moment before settling down. "If he did, then I would assume you have enough sense to take them as the ramblings of a drunk; one who has done plenty to distance himself from the church and almost nothing to support it."

The way Jeremy spoke bothered Annabelle terribly. He was typically one of the more obtuse people in her congregation, but this seemed a little overly defensive even for him. Annabelle frowned and looked up at the large crucifix mounted tall and proud on the altar table. She gazed at the figure of Jesus on the cross, thinking furiously. *What would you do now if you were me, boy-o?*

"How do you know Ted's a drunk? I thought you barely knew him?"

"I don't. Why are you asking so many questions?" Jeremy said, his smile disappearing and his tone shifting an octave lower, as deep and as powerful as a bass note. "I feel you are casting judgement upon me for some reason."

"No," Annabelle said. "I'm investigating a very serious matter in the parish. I need to be exact about every detail."

Jeremy pressed his thin lips tightly together. He placed his hands carefully on his knees as if meditating. Annabelle glanced at his long, extended fingers as he sat on his stool and wondered if such soft, delicate hands wielded the wrench that killed Mildred so brutally. She shook the thought away.

"Vicar," Jeremy said deliberately, "if there is something you wish to tell me, please do so. You are a woman of the cloth, after all. You have nothing to be afraid of."

Annabelle noticed something in Jeremy's eyes that she had never seen before. A hardness that seemed almost impenetrable. She'd never grown fully comfortable with the young man's awkward, reserved, and somewhat anti-social manner, but she hadn't felt intimidated or frightened by him until now. She stiffened her back, gathering her composure for a confrontation she anticipated would be deeply unsettling.

"Jeremy, I believe there's something you're not telling me. Something extremely important. In the short time you've been in Upton St. Mary, I've grown very fond of you, respectful of you, and in some ways, admiring of you, so it makes me deeply uncomfortable to talk in this way. But I'm certain that you are somehow involved in the disturbing events that have been occurring in the village, and I want you to tell me in what manner."

A wry smile played on Jeremy's lips. In the dim glow of the church light, and after her plea for an explanation, Annabelle found his amusement distressing.

"I have the greatest respect for you too, Vicar," said Jeremy, "as I do all those who dedicate their lives to the church. But I am surprised at the dogged determination with which you seek to know everything. Only He may know all things, and it is churlish and indolent of us to attempt His greatness. Was not Adam's aimless pursuit of knowledge man's first sin?"

Annabelle screwed up her face. She was accustomed to Jeremy's often annoying deference to scripture but this time he seemed to be wholly avoiding her questions.

"Jeremy, you know very well that I'm happy to engage in philosophical discussions with you at almost any time. We have had many productive, informative conversations. But right now, I beg you stick to the subject. Don't you understand how serious this matter is?"

"What are you talking about, Reverend?"

Annabelle could no longer beat about the bush. She had to speak plainly.

"We're talking about a person's death, Jeremy! A murder!"

Jeremy stood up. A half-foot taller than Annabelle, he cast an intimidating shadow over her. She took a small step back but kept a steely expression on her face.

"A death, indeed," Jeremy said, leaning over her. "And what is death but our day of judgement. The one we must all face. Death is sad, frightening, and to be avoided. But only by sinners. For the rest of us, for you and for me, Vicar, death is a glorious event."

CHAPTER TWENTY-FIVE

JEREMY TOOK A step towards her. Annabelle took two steps back. He was not her humble, reserved church organist anymore. There was a fire behind Jeremy's eyes. His lips curled with menace. His usually-hunched shoulders seemed broad and strong as he walked towards her, danger and purpose emanating from his being.

"What are you doing, Jeremy!?" Annabelle cried. "You're scaring me!"

"I know, Vicar," he said as he continued slowly towards her. "And that fact disappoints me greatly. A true follower of the Lord is never afraid. I've had my doubts about you for a long time. I fought my reservations, but I'm finally coming to accept them as the truth."

"What do you mean?" Annabelle shrieked as she stepped back into the aisle, keeping a healthy ten feet between them. "Jeremy! Stop!"

Unexpectedly, Jeremy obliged, his wry smile turning into a broad grin as he stood at the front of the church, even taller and scarier than before. Annabelle took the opportunity to gaze at him, still incredulous that this was the same man who asked so politely for a biscuit with his tea. The same man whose only goal, she had thought, was to play the best accompaniments to the psalms that he could.

"Tell me the truth, Jeremy," she said, too frightened for niceties and diplomacy. "Did you kill Mildred?"

After a few moments of stony-faced staring, Jeremy shook his head slowly. "No, I did not, Vicar." Annabelle let out the deep breath she had been holding in for seconds. *"God did."* Jeremy looked upwards with a beatific smile. It was as if he could see the heavens.

"What?" Annabelle sputtered with astonishment.

Jeremy slowly closed his eyes. He seemed rapt and blissful. He lowered his head then opened his eyes and looked at her.

"Did you know that Mildred was proud? Proud enough to pass judgement upon me? I know that I was a sinner, Vicar. Gambling is the resort of the scoundrel, the lowest of the low. I shall never forget the shame of indulging in such a pastime. But I repented. I prayed for strength from morning until night. I dedicated every ounce of myself, body and soul, to the Lord. I did everything I could to purge myself of that dreadful sin."

"So you *were* part of the gambling ring," Annabelle said, the words tumbling from her lips.

"I was. But I am a sinner no more."

"And Mildred found out?"

"My carelessness," Jeremy said, shifting his eyes to the door behind Annabelle. "She found my gambling book in my car." He turned back to her, his face now twisted with anger and bitterness. "My sin was great, but it didn't harm anyone, Vicar. Mildred, however, threatened to tell my grandmother. Can someone as reverent as you even comprehend such evil? To turn poor, sickly Nana's last days black with worry that her only grandchild, the source of everything good and pure in her life, had committed such sin? Isn't that blackmail?"

This time Annabelle stepped forwards, snarling with anger and resentment. "You killed Mildred because she found out about your *gambling?*" she cried.

Jeremy was unfazed. "As I told you before, Vicar," he said calmly, "I did not kill her. I am merely an instrument of God's will. I gave myself to Him long ago, and He has used me for many purposes since. Mildred's fate was in her own hands. Do not condemn the Lord for His just and Holy plans." Jeremy slowly picked up a tall, brass candlestick holder, one of two that stood on either side of the pulpit.

"Jeremy . . ." Annabelle warned, holding up her hand. "Whatever you're thinking of doing, don't. Please."

With a quick flick, Jeremy threw the candlestick holder into his other hand and smacked it into his palm like it was a baseball bat. He raised his eyes to the reverend, his broad grin now a focused smirk. He walked towards her.

"The Lord tried to warn Mildred," he said. "He first cast an affliction on her business, but she was too corrupt, too twisted by her own ego to see His truth." Jeremy was walking quickly now, quicker than Annabelle could retreat.

"Jeremy! Stop! Don't do this!"

"I am a conveyor of the Lord's light!" Jeremy cried in a voice Annabelle had never heard before. "I have given myself to Him entirely!"

Annabelle turned to the door, only a few feet away. She scuttled a few steps in fear, before tripping over her cassock. She fell to her knees. The vicar spun around quickly and saw Jeremy above her, tall and menacing. He wielded the candlestick holder above his head with both hands, ready to strike.

Annabelle had contemplated death many times, wondering what her last moments would be like, but she had never accounted for a death that would come so swiftly, so quickly, without even a moment in which to say a prayer. She cried out and shut her eyes tightly. There was a rush of air.

Thuds, grunts, and bizarre, animalistic snarling echoed around the church interior. Annabelle braced herself for an almighty bang and kept her eyes closed until she could stand it no longer. When the realisation dawned that she wasn't about to be released from this Earth, she tentatively opened her eyes.

Jeremy still loomed over her. He still clutched the candlestick holder above his head. He still had a murderous look in his eyes. But he had been prevented from striking Annabelle. For at the other end of the heavy, ornate candlestick, holding on for dear life, his face contorted with effort, was one Detective Inspector Michael Nicholls.

Jeremy and the inspector struggled, the weapon between them, both intent on defeating the other in this arduous tug-of-war. In contrast to this sharply male-on-male aggression, the puppy was at Jeremy's heels. She was yapping, jumping, and nipping, eager to take a piece out of his leg but not yet having quite the teeth to do so.

"Inspector!" Annabelle cried, her heart jumping.

As if spurred on by the sound of her voice, the inspector seemed to double in strength. He gripped the candlestick holder evermore firmly and used all his weight to lever it from Jeremy's large hands. The end of the candlestick holder hit the organist in the chest with a dull thump. Jeremy fell backwards onto the floor.

The inspector tore the makeshift weapon out of Jeremy's hands, and the puppy quickly seized her opportunity to contribute to Annabelle's rescue. She eagerly leapt onto Jeremy's chest, terrorising him as he scrambled on his back like an overturned beetle.

Tossing the candlestick roughly to one side, Nicholls forcefully lunged at Jeremy. The inspector flipped him over and snapped on a pair of handcuffs whilst the puppy snarled and nipped at Jeremy's long, elegant fingers.

The church organist struggled against his bonds, growling, furious at his capture. But his attempts were futile. Despite his best efforts to silence Annabelle forever, Jeremy, the seemingly pious, righteous, sanctimonious church organist, was caught.

CHAPTER TWENTY-SIX

NICHOLLS LEFT THE puppy to taunt Jeremy as she repeatedly pounced on his prone body whilst yipping in his ear. Quickly, he strode over to Annabelle, offering her his large, broad hand. She took it gratefully, and her saviour pulled her up, steadying her as she came to a stand.

"Oh!" Annabelle said, throwing her arms around him as soon as she was on her feet. "I thought I was finished! You saved me! Thank you, Inspector!"

Nicholls allowed himself a small smile as Annabelle hugged him tightly, though he contrived to make it vanish as soon as she pulled away.

"Are you alright, Reverend?" he asked, carefully studying her face.

Annabelle smiled at him. She was hugely relieved. "Thanks to my knight in shining armour," she said before looking over to the puppy, "and his fellow crusader."

The inspector took a deep breath. "What on earth happened?"

Annabelle looked at the inspector. Shaken and short of

breath, she found his stern, serious expression a source of comfort. "I believe you just stopped the murderer from striking again."

Nicholls looked at Jeremy, still squirming as the puppy jabbed her nose into his cheek. "Really? *Him?*" he said, his chest rapidly rising and falling as he recovered from his exertions.

"Inspector, you look more shaken than I am!"

"Of course, I'm shaken!" Nicholls cried, raising a hand to his stubble and rubbing it vigorously. "A second later and . . . well, who knows what would have happened!" He clasped Annabelle's arms. "Promise me you won't put yourself in such a dangerous situation ever again, Reverend!"

Annabelle smiled awkwardly. "I must say, Inspector, that's a rather strange reaction from a police detective!"

Nicholls released Annabelle and slowly smiled, chuckling some of his nerves away. "It's not, Reverend. It's the reaction of someone who's grown rather fond of you, despite your habit of pushing him to his very limits!"

Annabelle smiled broadly this time. "Perhaps it's *because* of that habit that he's grown fond of me."

"Perhaps, Reverend," Nicholls laughed. "Perhaps."

Two hours later, Annabelle sat in the inspector's office, recounting her perspective of the events for the third time to Constable Raven. They both stopped and turned their heads as Inspector Nicholls walked into the office behind his excited puppy.

"Unless your church organist was about to bake the biggest cake Upton St. Mary has ever seen, it's a pretty sure thing that he was the one behind the fuel tampering," the inspector said as he walked over to the chair behind his desk. "Thanks to my wet-nosed friend over there," he nodded at the puppy who was now tucking into her scraps in the corner of the room, "we found forty pounds of sugar and two unused fuel cans in his grandmother's house."

"*Your* wet-nosed friend?" Annabelle said.

Nicholls settled into his chair, shrugging his shoulders. "Raven, we found something in the home that may prove useful concerning this . . ." he quickly glanced at Annabelle, "gambling ring. Some directions—they seem to be in a sort of code—scribbled on the back of a beer mat."

The inspector pulled a plastic bag from his pocket. He leant across his desk to hand it to the constable, but Annabelle plucked it from his fingers. She gazed at the scrappy, stained card for a few moments before handing it over to the constable.

"They're directions to a pill box, an above-ground concrete bunker. They built many of them during the war as a line of defence in the event of an invasion. Soldiers could launch attacks from them, grenades, and such. There's a large one on the outskirts of the woods beside Shona Alexander's house," Annabelle said. "In the middle of the woods, there's a four-fingered tree that's a popular meeting spot for teenagers. If you walk in the direction of the shadows—assuming the gambling took place in the evening—you'll be heading east. You'll come across the pill box after a few minutes walk."

"She's right, sir. On this occasion, they must have done their gambling inside the bunker. I'll take this and put it with the other evidence." The constable left the office.

Nicholls turned and watched the puppy for a few moments, deep in thought, before shaking his head incredulously. "I still don't understand it," he said. "A young man.

A church organist. So good that he quits his job and moves halfway across England to tend to his sick grandmother. It's not a profile I see very often in killers."

"That was precisely why he did it," Annabelle said mournfully. "Jeremy had talent, youth, and the love of the whole community, but his only real passion, the thing he had based his entire identity on, was his 'goodness.' It's ironic, in a sense, that he did the most awful thing imaginable to hold on to the appearance of being completely beyond reproach, completely 'pure.' The Bible is full of stories in which the consequences of one small sin leads to the committing of many greater ones."

"My case reports are filled with many of the same stories," quipped the inspector.

"Almost all acts of violence are committed following a humiliation of some kind," Annabelle continued. "Among young men in particular. It's the only way many of them feel they can redress the balance and cancel out the shame."

Nicholls eyed the vicar, a humorous look in his eyes. "Are you considering a career in criminal psychology, Reverend?"

Annabelle chuckled. "It's certainly a fascinating subject."

"Well," Nicholls said, shuffling in his seat, "I'd much prefer studying it than engaging with it, to be honest. The real-life examples are a lot messier than the theories one finds in textbooks, that's for sure. When we dragged him in here, Jeremy told me everything like he was telling a bedtime story! No remorse, no sense of guilt or shame! Do you know, he waited outside the garage in the early morning on Saturday? He beat up Aziz on his way to work to put him out of the picture. He wore a balaclava so Aziz couldn't identify him. And, of course, no one would suspect the pure and righteous Jeremy right off the bat. He called Mildred to distract her and crept up behind her whilst they spoke on the phone. She couldn't even have looked him in the eye before he threw her in the pit, killed her, drove the car back over her, and put the keys back on the rack! I'd have to go back years to remember a case where somebody murdered their victim so clinically. It's . . . pretty distressing."

"Jeremy thought he was acting out God's will. He's obviously deeply troubled. His poor grandmother."

"And he was right under your nose the whole time," Nicholls said, a gently admonishing tone creeping into his voice. "In all the time he spent at the church, you didn't realise he was a psychopath?"

Annabelle pursed her lips. "Upton St. Mary is full of people with quirks and foibles. I always thought of him as slightly odd, of course, but . . ." She paused. "I suppose the idea was a little too close to home for me."

"You found it hard to believe someone so devout could be so dangerous?" Nicholls said.

Annabelle nodded. "Yes. Faith is a wonderful thing. It's difficult to witness it being used to justify such terrible deeds."

"He told me that he thought tampering with the fuel would convince Mildred that God was punishing her for threatening to expose him. He thought it would stop her. I'm not sure it's even faith at that point. Sounds more like madness."

Annabelle shook her head, still unable to fully believe what she now knew to be the truth. "It's so difficult to imagine that this was going on in Jeremy's life, and I didn't know anything about it. Just the idea of him *gambling* is hard to imagine, but to then encourage Mildred into keeping it a secret by trying to ruin her business . . . And then to *kill* her when that didn't work . . . You know, he must have come straight over to the church after murdering her. He sat there and played the organ as though it were a typical Saturday. I even spoke to him! I would never have guessed he had just committed cold-blooded murder."

"And assault," Nicholls added. "Don't forget about Aziz."

"Could he really be the one who attacked Aziz too?"

"He said he did, and I've all but confirmed it. We found Aziz's phone a little way down from the garage, he must have been holding it when he was attacked. There's a path that runs around the back of the garage leading to a small gap in the fence. Jeremy must have used it when he was contaminating the fuel. The thing is, Aziz also seems to have used it when walking to work. It makes a good shortcut if you're on foot, but only to the garage. Jeremy must have come upon him there. He probably pounced on Aziz before he knew what was happening. He couldn't have a fit, young lad come between him and what he had planned for Mildred. He presumably knew that Ted wouldn't be around, it being a Saturday morning."

"Oh my, it's so awful."

"When Aziz recovers, we'll talk to him and confirm it, though it's pretty much a foregone conclusion."

Annabelle sighed and placed her hands on the armrests of her chair to push herself out of it. She caught sight of the puppy snoozing in the corner, exhausted after her day's efforts.

"I suppose that's everything then, Inspector. I should get home. I'm desperately in need of a good night's sleep, although how I'll ever relax enough to drift off, I don't know." Annabelle stood up and walked to the door. She placed her hand on the doorknob.

"There was one more thing," the inspector said before Annabelle could leave. She turned around to look at him. "I'd prefer it if you called me Mike. It's not like you have any respect for my authority anyway," he added, grinning.

After laughing gently, Annabelle said, "In that case, I'd like you to call me Annabelle." The inspector nodded graciously. "I've always respected your humanity, Inspect—I mean, Mike. Perhaps this will help us relate on more equal terms."

Nicholls had an appreciative glint in his eye as he smiled at Annabelle. "Perhaps, Annabelle. Perhaps."

CHAPTER TWENTY-SEVEN

DESPITE THE COLD, wind-whipped rain and only the barest glimmer of light peeking through the grey clouds, almost half the village dropped by St. Mary's the following Saturday. When Annabelle had taken on her role as reverend in the Cornish countryside, she had introduced the celebration of the Winter Solstice to her parishioners. Solstice was an opportunity for all the villagers, no matter their faith, to generously show gratitude for their blessings by donating food items and other offerings to needy families just in time for Christmas. As a village full of cooks, bakers, and gardeners, Upton St. Mary was particularly well disposed towards anything culinary, and even more so when it involved sharing food with others.

Annabelle stood at the entrance to the church, offering her thanks as members of the community arrived. She watched as the villagers walked up the aisle to hand their donations to Philippa and Mrs. Applebury. The two women usually decorated the church with large, abundant floral displays but now put their skills to work showing off the villager's kindness with flourish and flair. The giant table at the front of the church was piled high with fruit, vegetables, pies, hams, poultry, joints of meat, cans, loaves of homemade bread, cakes, wine, and Christmas crackers. Spirits were high as the locals milled around talking, laughing, and smiling, enjoying the convivial atmosphere of the church.

"A far better turnout than last year," Philippa said as Annabelle walked up, "and it wasn't even raining then!"

Annabelle chuckled and nodded to a young child who walked up to proudly place a can of beans on top of the trembling table. The vicar pulled a bonbon from the open bag in her pocket. Stashing it there earlier had been a precautionary measure she had taken, knowing herself well enough to realise the sight and smell of so many baked goods would have her mouth watering.

"Well, I think this has lifted everyone's mood," Annabelle said as she looked around her. She sucked on the sweet before chewing and swallowing. "There hasn't been much cause for celebration in the village for a while now."

"Hmm," Philippa said. She had been shocked and appalled at the news of the gambling ring. "It's all well and good providing for the poor, and the Lord knows we have a few more needy families in the village this year but we're still nowhere near our goal for renovating the cemetery."

Annabelle turned to her beloved bookkeeper. "I'm sure we'll find a way, Philippa. We always do."

Philippa shrugged. The two women turned to look at the food table as they basked in the hum, chatter, and good humour that resonated inside the church's great stone walls.

"Is that . . . Ted?" Philippa said as a heavy-coated figure carrying multiple bags in each hand hustled his way through the doors.

"I believe it is," Annabelle replied, watching him bump his way through the crowd towards them.

"Hello, Vicar," Ted said. He placed his bags in front of the table and began taking cans and boxes from them. He placed his contributions on the table as Philippa slotted them artfully into the display.

"Hello, Ted," Annabelle said, mildly amused as he continued to pull from the seemingly bottomless bags. "Would you like some help?"

"Oh, no," Ted smiled, performing the task as though it were a complex mechanical manoeuvre requiring diligence and precision. He was out of breath. "I've got it."

"Where on earth did you get all this?" Philippa asked.

Ted looked up at the church secretary and smiled shyly. "I'm no cook," he said in between breaths. "And I don't grow anything. But that doesn't mean I shouldn't help."

"But I thought you were broke!" Philippa exclaimed.

Ted laughed and placed a few more items on the table before realising that there was no more space. He pushed the remaining donations underneath the table with his foot. "Actually," he said, "things are looking up for me."

"Oh?"

"Yes," he smiled. "I suppose you haven't heard. Apparently, Mildred left the garage to me in her will. I'm the new owner!"

"That's wonderful, Ted!" Annabelle exclaimed, clasping her hands together.

"How are you going to manage that?" Philippa said, not appearing quite so joyful. "You can't run a garage when you're hitting the sauce every night!"

"Philippa!" scolded Annabelle.

Ted laughed again. "No, she's right, Vicar. Owning a garage is a lot more responsibility than simply turning up and doing what the boss tells me. That's why I'm staying sober. No more pubs. No more gambling," he said, winking at Annabelle.

"I'm so happy to hear that!"

Ted nodded. "Well, I always said I just needed a lucky break. It doesn't get much luckier than suddenly being given your own garage." He looked sadly at the giant cross at the head of the church. "Mildred's still taking care of me, even now that she's gone. I owe her."

"I think she would be very proud of you," Philippa said, her reproachful tone softening. "She obviously thought you could do it. She wouldn't have left you the garage if she didn't."

"I won't be alone, of course," Ted added. "Aziz will still work with me, and he's a real talent, so it should make getting to grips with things a lot easier. That reminds me, Aziz wanted to thank you for helping him. He was going to come along, but he's got a lot of schoolwork to catch up on."

"I understand," Annabelle said. "How is he?"

"He's doing well. Recovering. He's a tough lad, more bothered about his studies than what happened."

"I'm glad to hear it," Annabelle said. "Take care, Ted."

"You too, Vicar," Ted said, turning away. "See you when your car breaks down!"

Annabelle laughed and watched Ted bustle his way down the aisle. On the way, he was drawn into conversation with Greg Bradley and Jenny McAllister just before he reached the doors.

"How about that?" Annabelle said.

"I don't care for surprises, myself," Philippa replied, "but there are some people for whom a shock does the world of good."

Annabelle looked at Philippa, acknowledging the wisdom of her words. "I do believe you're right."

Annabelle stood in the aisle for a few more minutes, thanking the villagers still streaming into the church with their donations. Philippa continued to help Mrs. Applebury arrange the overflowing pile that had now exceeded the table's capacity. Flowers, bunches of herbs, pots of honey and jam, chutneys, falafel, sweet and sour chicken, poppadoms, and naan bread spread across the floor, the front pews, and all around the base of the pulpit. Mr. Malik and his daughter Samira dropped by to donate some fine tobacco and a plate of Mrs. Malik's Florentine slices.

"How are you, Samira?"

"Very well, Reverend. I want to thank you for what you did for us, for Aziz."

"Hush, it was nothing. I'm glad to hear that he's doing well. What are your plans now?"

"I'm going to stay in the village until the new year, but then I'll be off back to uni. I'm looking forward to it."

"I hope you'll enjoy your few weeks with us. We'll miss you when you're gone."

The two women exchanged a hug, and Annabelle reciprocated Mr. Malik's slight bow with a hesitant and much deeper one of her own. She watched them walk proudly down the aisle and out into the rain.

As they left, Annabelle's eye was caught by an old man making his way into the church. He had a distinctive bow-legged gait. She knew him to be a rather isolated man who lived by himself in a secluded, decrepit farmhouse a little outside the village. Not much was known about him other than he enjoyed collecting war memorabilia and each Saturday he went to the pub to consume exactly two halves of bitter and a bag of peanuts in his favourite spot by the window.

It was not only the surprise of his visit that got

Annabelle's attention (she had never seen him in church before), but also what he was carrying. Rather than the plastic bags and cardboard boxes other villagers used to carry their donations, the elderly man's hand was tightly clenched around the thin handle of a flat, metal box, something that looked more appropriate for transporting tools than food.

Annabelle watched patiently as he ambled slowly towards her. After a rather long time during which she considered the possibilities of his visit, he stood in front of her and raised his bald, liver-spotted head to look at the vicar with his small, brown eyes.

"Hello."

"Hello, Mr. Austin. It's rather nice to see you in church."

Mr. Austin nodded slowly, as if the words took some time to reach him. He spoke again. "Can we talk somewhere private? Er . . . Miss?"

CHAPTER TWENTY-EIGHT

ANNABELLE CHUCKLED. "'REVEREND' is just fine, Mr. Austin. And of course, follow me."

She led the little man slowly off to the side where the church office was located. After opening the door for him and closing it behind her, Annabelle joined Mr. Austin as he stood beside the desk on which he had placed his peculiar case.

"So, what did you want to speak to me about, Mr. Austin?"

"I'd like to make a donation to the church."

"Oh! That's marvellous! Thank you very much. We're always grateful for such kindnesses." There was a few seconds pause before Mr. Austin nodded. He turned to the metal box, flipped the latch, and opened it.

"Golly gumdrops!" Annabelle cried loudly. She slapped her cheeks with her palms. She stared at the money that filled the entire case. Coins and notes of every denomination were scattered haphazardly.

"It's yours," Mr. Austin said calmly. "But I would like my box back."

"How much is in there?" It was all Annabelle could muster.

"A little over fifteen thousand pounds, I should say."

"Golly," Annabelle repeated, this time in a whisper. "Mr. Austin, where exactly did all this money come from?"

The old man's face remained impassive, but his eyes sparkled as he looked up at Annabelle. "Do you know anything about the card games that have been going on recently?"

Annabelle sighed. "I am rather more acquainted with those events than you would believe, Mr. Austin."

"Well," he said, gesturing at the money, "I'm a good card player."

Annabelle gawped at the man before her. With his sleepy appearance and innocent eyes, one could be forgiven for believing that he was the last person to possess a card maestro's wit and cunning.

"Do you mean to say that you won this money from those crook-ridden card games?"

Once again, Mr. Austin took a moment to answer, but when he did so, there was a mischievous quality to his voice. The words seemed to come from a man who had seen a lot and thought even more over the long decades of his lifetime.

"Card games are a simple matter of probability, Reverend. When you play with crooks, the probability is that someone is cheating. As I told you, I'm a good card player." Mr. Austin reached into the pocket of his brown slacks and pulled out a crumpled bag of bonbons, "but I'm even better at cheating."

It took a few seconds before Annabelle twigged, but when she did, her jaw dropped. Those were her bonbons! She searched her cassock for them but found her pockets empty. Mr. Austin held out the paper bag and winked. She took it slowly, stunned and speechless.

"How did you do that?" Annabelle said when she had recovered.

"Despite appearances," Mr. Austin began, "I am not from England. I was born in a far more unpleasant place. During the war, I had to make my way across Europe any way I knew how. I picked up a lot of skills on the road. Cards was one of them."

"Oh my!" Annabelle exclaimed. "That's quite a story!"

"It is no story," Mr. Austin said seriously. "It is my life. Which is why I usually prefer not to reveal such things."

"Of course," Annabelle said, quickly matching the old man's mood, "but I'm afraid I can't accept this money, Mr. Austin. It belongs to the men of Upton St. Mary. You should give it back."

"I already have," Mr. Austin replied. "This is what's left."

"You mean this is the money you took from the other men? The ones from outside the village?"

"Precisely."

Annabelle took a deep breath. She was struggling to keep up. "This money should go to the police," she said.

"No, it should not, Reverend," Mr. Austin replied. He was adamant. "This is my money, and it should go where I intend it. Now look, I've heard of your difficulties in raising funds for the cemetery, and at my stage of life, this is troubling. I'll be needing it myself soon. Upton St. Mary has been my home for many years. It's a place that has allowed me to live out my life in peace and solitude, just as I wished it. I am deeply indebted and grateful to this corner of the world, and it is my last wish that I be buried here. Now, if it makes you feel better, consider this a payment in advance for my eternal resting place, plus funeral expenses."

"But Mr. Austin—"

"I am an old man, Reverend. Old enough to be stubborn. Old enough to be taken on authority. Take this money, and fix the cemetery. If, when my time comes, it is unable to accommodate me, then I shall regard it as a promise broken."

"Mr.—"

"Goodbye, Reverend."

Mr. Austin's words were quick and strong, but the pace with which he turned and left Annabelle's office was anything but. Were Annabelle not so taken aback, she might have stopped him, but instead, she simply watched him amble out of the office in his uniquely awkward manner.

Once he was gone, Annabelle secured the money in the safe and took a few moments to gather herself before rejoining the others in the church. She emerged from the office beaming, and when she spied the inspector handing his gifts to Philippa, her smile grew even wider.

"Annabelle!" he called, relishing the informality of his greeting.

"Hello, Mike," Annabelle replied, emphasising his name. "I didn't expect you to still be in the village."

"Well," he said, leaning down to pet the puppy at his heel, "I was just clearing some things up before I take Molly here back to Truro."

"Molly! I like that name. Hello there, Molly!" Annabelle said, kneeling beside the inspector to scratch the dog's head.

Nicholls laughed as Molly licked Annabelle's hand. They stood up together.

"So," Annabelle began, "the gambling ring. You've broken it up? Is it all over?"

"The gambling? Absolutely. We caught them at it, and it didn't take much for those criminals to spill the dirt on each other. 'No honour among thieves,' and all that. As for the men in the village, we decided to let them go. Their wives will punish them much more effectively than the police ever could. I'm pretty sure none of them will go anywhere near so much as a betting shop ever again." Annabelle smiled at the inspector's good judgement.

"I am going to check into that Crawford character, though. I'd like to see what exactly he gets up to in that business of his. A gambling ring . . . Here in Upton St. Mary . . . I still can't believe it."

"I hate to say I told you so, but I was right."

"Yes, yes," the inspector said. "You've got to admit, though, at the time, it sounded ludicrous! A gambling ring! In Upton St. Mary?" he repeated. "Sometimes, Annabelle, you seem a little too ahead of us all when it comes to certain matters. If I didn't know better, I'd have suspected you were part of it. Or maybe you have a direct line to an all-knowing higher authority who gives you intel!"

Annabelle laughed heartily. "If that were true, I would be somewhere a lot sunnier and warmer than here!" she said, nodding at the pouring rain through the church's open doors.

Nicholls turned to watch the downpour, then looked back to the reverend with a small smile. "No, you wouldn't," he said quietly. "I doubt the crown jewels could tempt you away from this village."

Annabelle blushed a little as she gazed at the villagers attempting to gather sufficient gumption to brave the rain.

"There are more valuable things than riches, that's for sure," she said. "And the puppy? You're keeping her?"

The inspector's eyes softened when he looked down at his small, brown faithful friend. "Suppose I'll have to. Doesn't look like she wants to go anywhere, and I admit, she was pretty useful. I'll call James Paynton in the morning. Tell him I don't need one of his dogs after all."

Annabelle beamed with delight. The inspector looked at her, his eyes still soft, both of them seeming to consider the other in a different light.

"I hope it doesn't take a murder to bring you back to Upton St. Mary, Mike," Annabelle said, holding out her hand. Nicholls took it gently.

"Is that an invitation?"

Annabelle laughed lightly. "If you need one."

"Then I suppose we'll be seeing each other very soon."

"I look forward to it. Goodbye, Mike."

"Until next time, Annabelle."

Thank you for reading *Grave in the Garage*! I hope you love Annabelle as much as I do. Her adventures continue in *Horror in the Highlands* when Annabelle goes to visit her brother in Scotland. Will she see the inspector again?

A secluded island. A dark and stormy night. A treasure worth its weight in cake...

When a dead body is connected to a mysterious theft, it plunges the island's secretive community into chaos.

Annabelle is determined to find the killer, and expose the secret that threatens those she loves.

But with time running out, can Annabelle solve the mystery before the culprits strike again? Or before the islanders take matters into their own hands? Or will she need to call in reinforcements from the mainland in the shape of Inspector Nicholls? Get your copy of Horror in the Highlands from Amazon to find out! Horror in the Highlands is FREE in Kindle Unlimited.

To find out about new books, sign up for my newsletter: https://www.alisongolden.com

If you love the Reverend Annabelle series, you'll want to read the USA Today bestselling Inspector Graham series featuring a new and unusual detective with a phenomenal memory and a tragic past. The first in the series, *The Case of the Screaming Beauty* is available for purchase from Amazon and FREE in Kindle Unlimited..

And don't miss the Roxy Reinhardt mysteries. Will Roxy triumph after her life falls apart? She's sacked from her job, her boyfriend dumps her, she's out of money. So, on a whim, she goes on the trip of a lifetime to New Orleans, There, she gets mixed up in a Mardi Gras murder. *Things were going to be fine. They were, weren't they?* Get the first in the series,

Mardi Gras Madness from Amazon. Also FREE in Kindle Unlimited!

If you're looking for something edgy and dangerous, root for Diana Hunter as she seeks justice after a devastating crime destroys her family. Start following her journey in this non-stop series of suspense and action. The first book in the series, Snatched is available to buy on Amazon and is FREE in Kindle Unlimited.

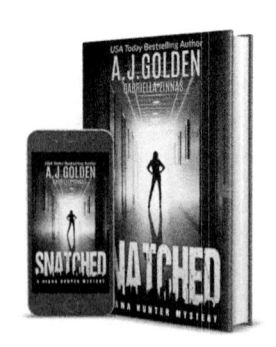

I hugely appreciate your help in spreading the word about *Grave in the Garage*, including telling a friend. Reviews help readers find books! Please leave a review on your favourite book site.

Turn the page for an excerpt from the next book in the Reverend Annabelle series, *Horror in the Highlands* . . .

A Reverend
Annabelle Dixon
Mystery

horror
in the
highlands

ALISON GOLDEN
JAMIE VOUGEOT

HORROR IN THE HIGHLANDS
CHAPTER ONE - FRIDAY

A SHORT, SHARP jolt woke Annabelle up, followed immediately by a queasy sensation of being gently rocked. She found herself grasping wildly for something with which to steady herself but succeeded only in banging her hand against the solid, cloth-covered wall next to her. After opening her eyes, Annabelle went stiff with surprise, struck by the realisation that this was not her cosy bed in her cosy cottage in her cosy adopted parish of Upton St. Mary.

Her confusion only lasted a few moments before the gentle chug of the train rolling along railway tracks, and the sparse, old-fashioned decoration of her sleeper cabin reminded Annabelle of where she was. Suddenly feeling entirely awake, Annabelle threw aside her sheet and leapt out of the narrow bed, quickly turning to the window. She furiously rubbed at the light mist on the glass and gazed through it intently. Her breath stopped, her eyes widened, and her heart began to sing as soon as she saw what lay on the other side of the thick glass. The beautiful Scottish Highlands!

Annabelle was on the Caledonian sleeper train on her

way from London to Inverness. She discovered the source of the rocky motions of her carriage when she saw that the train was winding itself along the crest of a riverbank, affording her an almost overwhelming view of the land unfurling ahead of her.

"Oh my!" gasped Annabelle as magnificent, dark-green hills tumbled elegantly among the thick mists of the spring morning. Faint traces of winter snow graced their highest points. Silver-clear water glistened as it made its way over the craggy rocks that lay nestled on the riverbed. Even the grey clouds above, dense and heavy, that threatened to burst forth at any moment, somehow seemed joyous to her. It had been over a year since she last visited Scotland, and although she remembered well how impressed she always was by the highland landscape, memories alone could not capture such magnificence.

Annabelle had grown accustomed to the quiet, natural beauty of her parish in Upton St. Mary. It was delicate and garden-like. Down there, spring was a time of blossoming colour and light breezes that made the budding, sprouting, emerging flora dance cheerfully. Here, however, there was no light breeze. Thistles and nettles stood defiantly, sturdy and proud against the strong winds and heavy rains. One need only look at their surroundings to see why the Scots had a reputation for being a tough bunch. Demonstrations of courage and fortitude were all around them.

Whilst Annabelle was basking in the glorious scenery, she said a quiet, humble prayer and set about getting dressed. She still had a long way to go; there was yet another train journey and two ferries to catch before she reached her journey's end.

Once ready, she picked up her heavy sports bag and made her way to the lounge car where she quickly secured herself a cup of hot tea and a comfortable seat from which to contemplate the view. It was an intimate carriage, and already a few early risers were enjoying their breakfasts. Annabelle glanced around and was greeted with quiet smiles and deferential nods, attracting instinctive respect despite wearing her regular clothes instead of her customary cassock.

It struck her that only a particular type of traveler still took the train to Scotland. A garishly-coloured plane could take one most of the way in a tenth of the time for the same price. A leisurely drive whilst enjoying frequent pit stops and the company of friends or family, even unswerving solitude, was another alternative. As she sat at her table, it seemed to Annabelle that only those with a very contemplative, appreciative, and patient disposition would choose the train as their preferred mode of transport. It was this group that Annabelle was happiest to place herself among.

She sipped from her teacup and reached down into her sports bag for the oatcakes Philippa had prepared for her. As she pulled the foil-wrapped package out of her bag, she could almost hear the voice of her church secretary fussing. *"I don't care if they do serve food on the train! It'll be far too expensive and five days old anyway!"*

Annabelle smiled as she delicately nibbled before furtively pushing an entire oatcake into her mouth. She brushed the crumbs from her fingers and sipped the last of her tea. Reaching deeper into her bag, Annabelle pulled out the gifts she had procured for the two people who were the reason for this long journey; the two people she loved most in the world, her older brother, Roger, and his daughter, Bonnie.

The first gift was a hand-knitted scarf in red and white, the colours of Arsenal football club, her brother's singular passion since he was a boy growing up in the East End of London. The scarf had been knitted by Mrs. Chamberlain, who lived just around the corner from St. Mary's Church, and who seemed to Annabelle to possess hands imbued with the dexterity of a concert pianist and the flight of a hummingbird. A computer analyst who worked from home, Roger still kept abreast of every fixture and transfer dealing his beloved team was involved in. Annabelle knew the gift would be appreciated, especially on the blustery moors of Blodraigh, the outer Scottish island where he and Bonnie lived.

Roger was a single dad, a widower. His daughter was seven years old. Annabelle had visited her niece almost every spring since her mother's death when Bonnie was a baby. Now as Annabelle watched the young girl grow ever more confident, energetic, and tall, her visits had become one of the year's highlights for both of them. Annabelle adored her niece, finding in her a kindred spirit who loved sweets and laughter as much as she did, whilst Bonnie, growing up on the rather barren and isolated island, thought her aunt terribly exotic.

Bonnie longed to hear tale after tale of what, to her, were the peculiar and far-off people and events of Upton St. Mary. To the young girl, almost anything beyond the coastline of the island she had grown up on was the source of mystery, excitement, and intense curiosity. She bombarded her aunt with question after question on the smallest of details. She asked about the types of plants and flowers that surrounded St. Mary's church, the shops people frequented, and the fashions and foibles particular to those who lived on the south coast. Annabelle indulged her niece's inquisitions, finding Bonnie a rapt audience for her accounts of life as an English country vicar.

Nevertheless, even though Annabelle did her best to temper the wide-eyed wonder that accompanied her answers to Bonnie's questions, it often seemed that Bonnie envisioned Upton St. Mary as a bustling metropolis of momentum and action; a place in which people were determined and always in a hurry; where there was drama and excitement on a regular basis. Whenever Annabelle was tempted to dissuade Bonnie of these notions and convince her that Upton St. Mary was only slightly larger and busier than Blodraigh, she saw her stories through the young girl's eyes, and it dawned on her that her own life as the vicar of the village was indeed rather hectic and often full of surprises.

Bonnie loved nothing more than adventure, and she dreamed constantly of an escape from her narrow existence. It was for that reason (as well as a rather obvious hint in one of Bonnie's letters) that Annabelle had brought her a special, limited-edition copy of the latest book in the hottest children's fantasy series, *Celestius Prophesy and the Circle of Doom*. It had been released only a few days prior, and Annabelle had reserved it long in advance, cherishing the moment she would hand it to her niece.

Annabelle set about wrapping the presents in the paper she had bought during her stopover in London. As she did so, she glanced at the passing lochs and mountains, a sense of satisfaction warming her insides like a glowing hearth. Upton St. Mary may not be a hive of activity and drama but the persistent requests and quirks of her congregation still kept her busy. It was appealing, exciting, essential even, to squirrel oneself away from those demands every so often. As she always did, Annabelle had agreed to give a sermon at the local church during her stay on the island, but it would be her only duty. For the rest of her week-long visit, she was determined to enjoy the rest and tranquility that her trip would offer her. What could possibly be more pleasing than spending time with her much-loved brother and his daughter amidst the serene and beautiful landscape of a Scottish island?

To get your copy of *Horror in the Highlands* visit the link below:
https://www.alisongolden.com/horror-in-the-highlands

REVERENTIAL RECIPES

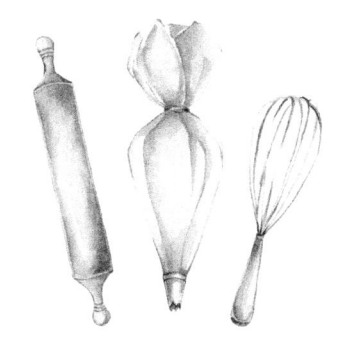

Continue on to check out the recipes for goodies featured in this book...

MIRACULOUS ENGLISH MADELINES

For the madeleines
1 stick (115g) butter, softened
½ cup (100g) sugar
2 eggs, beaten
½ cup (60g) flour
1 ½ tsp baking powder
¼ tsp salt
1 tsp warm water

To finish
2 - 4 tbsp red fruit jam
4 tbsp shredded coconut
6 candied cherries, halved

Preheat the oven to 180°C/350°F/Gas mark 4. Grease 6-8 dariole (pudding) moulds with butter and dust with flour.

Cream together the butter and sugar in a mixing bowl until light and fluffy, using an electric or rotary beater or wooden spoon. Beat in the eggs.

Sieve the flour with the baking powder and salt. Stir in

1 tablespoon of flour into the butter mixture until well mixed. Gradually fold in the remaining flour. Add enough water to give the mixture a soft, dropping consistency.

Divide the mixture equally between dariole moulds. Bake for 15 to 20 minutes or until well-risen and golden.

Turn the madeleines carefully out of the moulds, upside down, and leave to cool. Trim the bases if they do not stand up well. When cool, brush with the sieved jelly, then roll in the coconut. Stand upright on a serving plate and decorate the top of each with a halved candied cherry.

Makes 6 to 8.

VENERABLE VICTORIA SANDWICH

For the sponge cake:
1 cup sugar
1 ½ sticks butter
3 eggs, beaten
1 ½ cups flour
2 ¼ teaspoons baking powder
¼ + ⅛ teaspoons salt
2 tablespoons warm water
Strawberry jelly for spreading

For the glacé icing:
1 ¼ cups powdered sugar
1-2 tablespoons warm water
Walnut halves for decoration

Preheat the oven to 190°C/375°F/Gas mark 5. Grease two 18cm/7-inch sandwich tins and dust with flour.

Cream together the sugar and butter in a mixing bowl until light and fluffy, using an electric beater or wooden spoon. Gradually beat in the eggs.

Sift the flour, baking powder, and salt. Stir 1 tablespoon of flour into the butter mixture until well mixed. Gradually fold in the remaining flour. Add enough water to give the mixture a soft, dropping consistency. Pour into sandwich tins.

Bake just above the centre of the oven for about 20 minutes or until well-risen and golden, and the cakes have shrunk away from the sides of the baking tins.

Turn out onto a wire rack and leave to cool. Spread the jam evenly over one cake and place the remaining cake on top.

To prepare the icing, sift the icing sugar into a mixing bowl. Gradually mix in the water until a smooth paste is formed. It should coat the back of the spoon. Quickly beat out any lumps. Spread over the cake before the icing is set, and decorate around the edge with your decoration.

Serves 8 – 10.

MARVELLOUS MERINGUES

2 egg whites
4 oz (120g) fine sugar
A little fine sugar for dredging
1 cup (240g) of whipping cream, whisked to stiffness

Preheat the oven to 120°C/225°F/Gas mark 1. Put the egg whites in a large mixing bowl and beat until stiff with a balloon whisk, rotary, or electric beater. Fold in 1 tablespoon of the sugar, then beat again until smooth and satiny. It should stand in peaks. Fold in the remaining sugar with a large metal spoon.

Put the meringue mixture into an icing bag fitted with a 1.25cm/½-inch plain pipe. Pipe into small rounds on baking paper placed on a baking sheet. Dredge with a little sugar.

Bake in the oven for 1 to 2 hours or until the meringues are crisp and firm to the touch. If the meringues begin to turn brown, open the oven door slightly.

Remove from the oven, and leave to cool on a wire rack. Peel off the paper when the meringues are completely cold, and sandwich together with the whipped cream just before serving.

Makes approximately 6.

Notes

Meringues are easy to make if a few basic rules are followed. Make sure all your equipment is grease-free. Use 60g/2 ounces of fine sugar for every egg white. Refrigerate the egg whites for 24 hours before using. Do not over beat once the sugar is added. Bake at a very low temperature.

FLAMING FLORENTINE SLICES

---

12 oz (340g) of semi-sweet baking chocolate, broken into pieces, or chips
½ stick (55g) of butter
½ cup (100G) brown sugar
1 egg, beaten
2 oz (60G) of mixed dried fruit
1 cup (80G) finely shredded coconut
2 oz (60G) of candied cherries, quartered

Preheat the oven to 150°C/300°F/Gas mark 3. Put the chocolate pieces in a heatproof bowl, and stand it over a pan of hot water until melted, stirring occasionally. Spoon the chocolate into a greased 20cm/8-inch square cake tin or silicone baking pan. Spread out over the bottom and leave to set.

Meanwhile, cream together the butter and sugar until the mixture is light and fluffy. Beat in the egg thoroughly. Mix together the remaining ingredients and add to the creamed mixture. Spoon into the tin and spread over the set chocolate.

Bake in the centre of the oven for 40 to 45 minutes, or until golden-brown. Remove from the oven and leave for 5 minutes, then carefully mark into squares with a sharp knife. The mixture will be quite sticky at this stage.

Leave until cold, then loosen with a palette knife and lift carefully from the tin. Cut into squares.

Makes 12 to 16.

All ingredients are available from your local store or online retailer.

You can find printable versions of these recipes at www.alisongolden.com/ggrecipes

"Your emails seem to come on days when I need to read them because they are so upbeat."
- Linda W -

For a limited time, you can get the first books in each of my series - *Chaos in Cambridge, Hunted* (exclusively for subscribers - not available anywhere else), *The Case of the Screaming Beauty,* and *Mardi Gras Madness* - plus updates about new releases, promotions, and other Insider exclusives, by signing up for my mailing list at:

https://www.alisongolden.com/annabelle

TAKE MY QUIZ

What kind of mystery reader are you? Take my thirty second quiz to find out!

https://www.alisongolden.com/quiz

BOOKS IN THE REVEREND ANNABELLE DIXON SERIES

Chaos in Cambridge (Prequel)

Death at the Café

Murder at the Mansion

Body in the Woods

Grave in the Garage

Horror in the Highlands

Killer at the Cult

Fireworks in France

Witches at the Wedding

COLLECTIONS

Books 1-4

Death at the Café

Murder at the Mansion

Body in the Woods

Grave in the Garage

Books 5-7

Horror in the Highlands

Killer at the Cult

Fireworks in France

ALSO BY ALISON GOLDEN

FEATURING INSPECTOR DAVID GRAHAM

The Case of the Screaming Beauty

The Case of the Hidden Flame

The Case of the Fallen Hero

The Case of the Broken Doll

The Case of the Missing Letter

The Case of the Pretty Lady

The Case of the Forsaken Child

The Case of Sampson's Leap

The Case of the Uncommon Witness

FEATURING ROXY REINHARDT

Mardi Gras Madness

New Orleans Nightmare

Louisiana Lies

Cajun Catastrophe

As A. J. Golden

FEATURING DIANA HUNTER

Hunted (Prequel)

Snatched

Stolen

Chopped

Exposed

ABOUT THE AUTHOR

Alison Golden is the *USA Today* bestselling author of the Inspector David Graham mysteries, a traditional British detective series, and two cozy mystery series featuring main characters Reverend Annabelle Dixon and Roxy Reinhardt. As A. J. Golden, she writes the Diana Hunter thriller series.

Alison was raised in Bedfordshire, England. Her aim is to write stories that are designed to entertain, amuse, and calm. Her approach is to combine creative ideas with excellent writing and edit, edit, edit. Alison's mission is simple: To write excellent books that have readers clamouring for more.

Alison is based in the San Francisco Bay Area with her husband and twin sons. She splits her time between London and San Francisco.

For up-to-date promotions and release dates of upcoming books, sign up for the latest news here: https://alisongolden.com/annabelle.

For more information:
www.alisongolden.com
alison@alisongolden.com

- facebook.com/alisongolden.books
- twitter.com/alisonjgolden
- instagram.com/alisonjgolden

THANK YOU

Thank you for taking the time to read *Grave in the Garage*. If you enjoyed it, please consider telling your friends or posting a short review. Word of mouth is an author's best friend and very much appreciated.
Thank you,

Printed in Great Britain
by Amazon